The Soul's Motivation

Book #2 of the *Men of 1302* Series

Dante D. Long

The Soul's Motivation

Copyright © 2017 by Dante D. Long

www.darkdiamondbooks.com/author_dante.html

Dark Diamond Publishing, LLC.

Book Cover Art by: Darien Pitts
Edited by: Herwritehand Publishing,
http://www.herwritehand.com

ISBN: 9780989578042

www.darkdiamondbooks.com

Printed in the United States of America

PUBLISHER'S NOTE

To my fans and friends that have supported
me from the very beginning and
to all past, present, and future
Servicemembers of the
United States Armed Forces

The

Soul's

Motivation

Prologue

What goes on in the mind of a Soldier as he prepares for war? Fear and eagerness of the unknown is definitely sure to creep in. Some focus on the fact that death may be looming and indulge in as much as of the pleasures that most take for granted. Others focus on what is really important to them and cherish those that love and support them. One may question his or her military training. Despite how new or how experienced a Soldier may be, there is a sense of nervousness that is always apparent.

Second Lieutenant Kyle Scott was experiencing all of those emotions and some. After graduation from the Military Intelligence Officer Basic Course in Fort Huachuca, he made the trek back to Georgia where he grew up. He had just spent a few days hanging out with his friends, Jasper and Rodney from Pembrook College.

Jasper was still mentally recovering from a robbery attempt that went wrong, which was instigated by his ex-fiancé, Tina. Multiple people, including Tina, went to jail afterwards, and Jasper was left confused and attempted to mend his broken heart. His budding career at InfoTech Solutions kept him busy during the day, and he was busy most nights in the arms of another woman … actually several women.

Rodney's band, Dipped in Soul, continued to gain popularity in the Memphis and Arkansas areas. As the new leader, he reinvented the band's sound into something unique and exciting. Opting to drop out of Pembrook to take care of his wife and young child, he worked tirelessly to make ends meet and save for tuition. He wanted to one day join his former roommates and become an alumnus of the historical black university.

Kyle often referenced interactions with Jasper and Rodney over the years. He would keep those memories with him always, and they would comfort him in the months to come. He was about to arrive to a new Army unit just in time to finish training and other preparations and deploy to Iraq. The transition from college student to military professional was Kyle's most important mission that he did not take lightly.

Chapter 1

September 23, 2002

Kyle's heart always seemed to skip a beat every time he crossed the Georgia state line. His eyes could be closed, and he would still feel something in his soul signifying that he just passed the large "Welcome to Georgia" sign. It felt good for him to be almost home. His father, Retired Colonel Reginald Kyle Scott, used to tell him in college, "Remember this…you can never go home again." Kyle never understood what he meant, but he was about to find out during his short visit with his parents. Afterward, he'd report for duty at Fort Stewart, Georgia the following Monday.

Earlier that day, he left his old college roommate's apartment near Memphis, Tennessee with a car packed full of his civilian clothes, Army uniforms, and other stuff that he could cram into it.

He shook hands and hugged Jasper after loading his book bag, and said, "Thanks for everything, brother. You going to be ok?"

Jasper looked down for a second before replying. He was not in the mood to talk about the drama that had recently transpired due to his ex-fiancé. "Mane, I'm straight. More importantly, are you going to be ok, soldier boy?"

Kyle, always one to be stolid, looked at his homeboy and quickly replied, "Yep." On the inside, he wanted to tell Jasper about his nightmares and overthinking that led to many sleepless nights. His pride wouldn't let him, and his face showed no signs of worry.

After a few more minutes of small talk, they both hopped in their respective cars and left Jasper's apartment complex. Kyle followed as Jasper led him to the highway that he would need to travel to head toward Birmingham, Alabama. As Kyle neared the exit, he could see Jasper signaling to him to get ready to veer to the right lane. Seconds later, Kyle honked his car horn and drove up the ramp. He looked over to see Jasper's profile and realized again that he would not see him again for a year or more.

After stopping shortly for a quick bathroom break and to refuel, Kyle called his dad before driving the final stretch to his parents' home in Alpharetta, a suburb of Atlanta. To commemorate his arrival back to Georgia, he popped in a cassette tape with a mix of his favorite booty-shake music. His favorite song, "Baby, Baby" by Kilo Ali, kicked in with too much bass for the factory speakers in his car. The song always improved his mood. That and his mom's cooking were enough to wake him from the fatigue of his six hour drive.

He was looking forward to being back in Georgia for a while. The last time that he visited home was the Thanksgiving before his Pembrook College graduation the previous May. He had seen both of his parents at his college graduation, and he recently saw his dad at his graduation from his officer's course. His classmates were in awe to see that he was the son of a highly decorated and retired officer. Kyle, on the other hand, was embarrassed by all the phoniness and politicking done during the graduation, which his dad often partook.

As he neared his parent's house, he lowered the volume of his music and rolled down the window to feel the Georgia air blow into the car. Though it was late September, the air was still quite humid and hot. He pulled up around 2:40 p.m., excited yet ready to take a nap.

After a few hugs from both parents, he dropped off his bags in his old bedroom. He looked through some unopened mail on his bed before heading downstairs to get some of his mom's cooking. He noticed that some of his old artifacts were moved around, but he just attributed it to his parents probably cleaning up before his arrival.

He avoided any talk with his father that dealt with military operations and his upcoming deployment. He focused on making his plate of food and discussing the heavy construction on highway 285. While Kyle was eating, his cellphone rang. He answered it without even knowing who was calling. "Hello."

"Wassup playa, playa?" the female voice roared into his earpiece. "You can't call your friend and let me know you made it to town? Oh, my bad. I meant to say, sir, you failed to call and report your presence, sir!" She busted into laughter, "Is that how you guys say it?"

Kyle chuckled at how his childhood friend, Mia, tried to mimic military jargon. "No, you are the playa, Mia! You know how you do. Why you trying to talk all Army and stuff? It sounds weird."

"Shiiit, sir, yes sir. You going to come over and give me some demerits or something, Kyle sir? If you do, wear your uniform…shiit. You won't have to wear it long. "

"Mia, get on with that…mess." He almost cursed instead of saying mess, but looked up to see his smiling mother staring at him as soon as she heard Mia's name. Kyle's mother always suggested that Mia was a great catch for companionship and constantly parroted her educational stats, job position, beauty, and other things.

Mia went to Spelman and Georgia Tech in a dual school engineering degree program. She was currently working for General Electronics as a Quality Control Engineer. She and Kyle played with the idea of dating, but distance and the possibility that their mostly physical relationship would change the friendship for the worst, pushed them to deciding to just be friends without benefits. Kyle never wavered from that decision, but Mia occasionally dropped hints that she was open to exploring their physical past again and more if he allowed.

Mia and Kyle talked for a few minutes more as he stuffed his mouth and agreed to discuss visitation plans once he was settled and got some rest. Opposite of his actions earlier, he addressed his father with a random question of Army regulations as he hung up the phone to avoid his mother talking about Mia. As expected, his father proudly boasted his procedural and doctrinal knowledge, sprinkled with historical accounts and opinionated suggestions. Kyle simply said, "Um huh," and continued his meal.

After his meal and nap, Kyle woke up around 7 p.m. but was still groggy from his drive. Despite his state of fatigue, he was determined to hit the streets. He would only be in town for a few days, and he wanted to make them count. He promised Mia that he would come over, but he was looking forward to hanging out with some of his fraternity brothers too. Most of his childhood friends pledged the same fraternity in college, and the common bond they all shared only deepened their friendships.

After a quick shower and ironing some clothes that he pre-starched before his nap, he called Mia to announce that he was coming over the next day. He wanted her to meet him and his boys. He thought to himself that he should probably grab a three pack of condoms on his way at a local gas station. The condoms would come in handy in case he didn't trust himself around his friend or if he was convinced to let go of his previous vow. Mia could be very forceful.

He made his way downstairs and made a quick sandwich in his parent's kitchen. He was supposed to go out with his friends to grab a bite to eat, but he wanted something on his stomach in case some serious liquor drinking came first upon his arrival. He called Mia to meet him at the restaurant, Corazon

Roto Bar and Grill around 8:30 p.m. and his homeboys were supposed to arrive around nine.

Kyle wanted to talk to Mia before engaging in the typical shit-talking that was destined to ensue once Greg and Lamari arrived. Mia didn't particularly get along with those two and would probably leave early after having tolerated them for so long. Kyle wanted to discuss the new lady in his life and get his home girl's input before the fellas arrived. Other than being forceful, she was also known for being brutally honest.

Mia Stanley was known to make an entrance, and her arrival to the Corazon Roto was no different. She walked through the door talking on her phone wearing form fitting jeans and a long white tee shirt, with bright red knee high boots and red lipstick to match. Kyle noticed, just like everyone else in the spot, that she was purposely walking slowly to garner as many looks as possible. He also noticed that she had gained a few pounds since he last saw her, but her booty was just as he remembered it. That part of her always made him reconsider her advances . . . every time.

"Kyle, you betta get up and give your girl a hug. One of these girls up in here may give you some after seeing you do that...since you don't want me." Kyle just smiled as he rose to hug her. "You like my outfit? I figured that I would wear red and look like a groupie with you and your frat brothers."

"I see you, pimp! Looking good, pimp." Kyle ignored her comment about not wanting her as well as her longer than usual embrace. "Lamari and Greg should be here soon."

"Fuck them, ok? I came to see you. Shiiit...that Army stuff got you all swole and shit." Kyle knew that he was being undressed mentally by his friend, and he had to adjust himself in his slacks for he was tempted to be undressed. He played it cool and went on to call over the waitress to order the first round of drinks.

After some basic conversation about career and life, Mia decided to cut to the chase before Kyle opened up about it. "So...ummm...who you fucking while you are in town?" He flinched at how loudly she said it as the music in the place had lowered during the transition to the next song in the playlist playing. "I know you are home and about to call up someone while you are here. It better not be that trifling heifer, Briana or that flat booty bitch you used to hit, Angie."

Like he was jumping double-dutch, Kyle patiently waited to get a word in as she continued her rant trying to get into his business. Once she realized that he was not saying anything, she quieted and said, "So?" He took a deep breath and took a sip of the Long Island Iced Tea that he was drinking. She glared at him, and repeated, "So?"

It was always weird to Kyle that Mia seemed concerned about his love life, often listening attentively and offering advice over the years. She genuinely cared for his happiness, but she had no issue reminding him that he could have been with her. She often said things like, *"If you would have been with me, you wouldn't have to fuck with these crazy ass heifers all the time."*

"Well, actually, I am seeing someone. Her name is Raven. I met the young lady while I was at Fort Huachuca. We were study partners during the course, and…"

Mia interrupted, "I already don't like the bitch . . . I mean, young lady. Only your ass calls women 'young lady'." Kyle only laughed because he wasn't offended at his lady friend being called a bitch. He knew that is just how Mia talked. "I'm sorry, sir. Please continue."

He continued, "Thank you. Like I was saying, we were study partners, and things just kinda…happened." Mia didn't respond as he kept talking. "You know that I don't usually fall for anyone quickly. Logically, it doesn't make sense to try to date someone before I deploy, but...."

Mia interrupted again, "But you going to do it anyway? Well, be careful. Is she going to be at the same Army base as you?"

In his deep, monotone voice, he simply replied, "Nope." He then took another sip of his drink and waited for Mia to keep going.

"So you barely know the bitch...my bad, young lady...and you going to be dating her long distance?" Mia was always concerned about Kyle's choices of female companions, but she saw a lot of red flags in her mind regarding Raven. Once, he didn't respond, she ended that part of the conversation with, "Aight, playa...aight."

She wanted to say more, but she spotted Lamari and Greg walking through the door wearing frat shirts as she expected. She looked at Kyle and said, "You see. That is why I wore what I wore. Your boys are here."

The friendships that Kyle had with the two suave gentlemen was similar to that which he had with Jasper and Rodney. It was like the latter two were somewhat like replacements for his childhood buddies, but it was very different in so many ways. He even mentally compared Jasper to Greg several times in the past. They were like two versions of the same person.

As all the men greeted each other with hugs and covered up fraternal handshakes, Mia sat and waved at the two who just joined them. Greg winked at Mia, and she rolled her eyes in response. Lamari's first words were, "Frat, your dad be up in the meetings trying to run everything." Kyle and his father belonged to the same fraternity. It was another point of pride for Kyle's father; it was as if his son was following his footsteps in multiple aspects.

After the greetings, everyone ordered appetizers and drinks. Then they conversed about various topics. They talked about the war and Kyle's upcoming deployment as well as fraternity stuff and past episodes of their youth. Mia decided to stay for the duration because she wanted to hang out with her longtime buddy. She ignored Greg's flirtatious and suggestive statements, which got bolder as the drinking and eating continued. Kyle never intervened because he knew she could handle herself.

At some point in the conversation, Greg asked, "Are you going to let your ex-girlfriend, Briana, see you while you are in town?" Mia grunted loudly upon hearing Briana's name, and Greg laughed.

Kyle paused and said, "Nope."

Honestly, Kyle thought about it, but he figured it would be best if he didn't open that closed part of his past again. They met up for one last sexual encounter before he went to Fort Huachuca after graduation. It was obvious that Briana wanted more after seeing his potential that she once overlooked in high school. That is how Kyle understood her feelings to be.

Mia expressed her disapproval of Kyle hooking up with Briana in case he was thinking about it. Laughter erupted from the guys sitting with her, which was loud enough for most of the other patrons in the restaurant to hear.

Lamari told Kyle, "Big man, it's good to see you again."

Kyle smile and said, "Yep, it's good to see you guys, too."

Chapter 2

The dream always started off the same. Kyle was in a staff meeting, in some barracks-style meeting room, the walls covered with maps of Iraq. The same faceless Army officer, the insignia on his collar showed the rank of Captain, droned on about some report he gave to the faceless Commander. As the Captain finished talking, the Commander turns to look at Kyle and says, "Ok, Lieutenant Scott. Tell us what you think."

As the dream continues, Kyle confidently reported proposed enemy cells, explained enemy trends, and gave recommendations about possible enemy targets to build operational scenarios. After Kyle's report, each time, the faceless Commander would applaud and tell him, "Good work, Lieutenant Scott. Good work." The other members of the staff would congratulate him and cheer as he returned to his seat.

Later in the dream, Kyle realizes that his assessment was totally inaccurate and causes a mission to fail miserably. He sees his Commander cursing him out in a small office space while throwing stuff at him for being wrong *again*. The dream always ends differently after Kyle is chewed out by his Commander. Sometimes, the dream would end with him at the funeral of a faceless Soldier. The Soldier's death was a result of his inaccurate intelligence assessment. Other times, Kyle was captured by the very men who he reported as enemies. Then sometimes he would be staring at the faceless dead who he thought were the bad guys, but were actually innocent. The true bad guys got away only to terrorize another day.

The dreams, more like nightmares, started shortly after he received a phone call from his future Commander, LTC Bloomberg, while he was at training in Arizona. The nightmares had gotten worse the closer it got to his arrival at Fort Stewart. Sometimes the nightmares woke him up out of his sleep, and then sometimes they didn't.

Kyle awoke, tired and somewhat dehydrated, from an unrestful night plagued with his usual nightmare. He wanted to go for a run, but chose to sleep in a little longer to make up for his lack of sleep. He felt sorry for the crew that he hung out with the night before considering the amount that they all drank. The difference between Kyle and the crew was that he didn't have to go to work the next morning. He checked his text messages and slowly moved downstairs after having used the bathroom.

He knew his mom was downstairs cooking type of the breakfast that she usually only cooked on weekends consisting of grits, scrambled eggs with cheese, homemade biscuits, and thick cut, peppered bacon that you can only get at the nearby butcher's. His mom had been going to that particular butcher for years to get what Kyle affectionately called "mama" bacon. It wasn't the weekend, it was Tuesday, but she wanted to be make her son's short visit as special as possible. As any mother would be, she was scared about the journey that her boy was about to embark upon. She had gone through similar feelings when her husband used to deploy during his time in the service, but it was different for her when her only child was ordered to go.

"Good morning, mom." Kyle spoke to his southern belle mother and sat down at the table. He always felt that she was the perfect wife for an Army officer. She was supportive and strong enough to handle business when his dad wasn't around. Kyle's father used to work late in the office, or would be conducting field training exercises for weeks. Other times, he would have to deploy to various parts of the world without much notice.

His mother fixed his plate and asked about his night as she brought it to the table. "How did you sleep last night? How did things go with Mia?" Kyle came home around midnight, and she assumed that he was with Mia the whole time.

"Lamari, Greg, Mia, and I hung out at that new restaurant on Peachtree. It was cool." Small talk continued about the night before while they ate. He wanted to tell his mom about the nightmares that he was having, but he chose not to to prevent instigating further worry about his upcoming deployment. He hoped that his mom wouldn't bring up, the "give Mia a chance" speech, but without fail, as soon as he got up to get another bowl of grits, she brought up the subject. He figured it was probably time to mention that he was seeing someone, and reiterate that Mia was just a friend.

"Ma, you know I am still seeing that girl in my class that I told you about?"

She figured as much, but Mia really impressed her. She wanted the next step in the typical progression of a young military officer after commissioning which was for him to find a wife and have kids. She knew how picky her son was and figured that his choice was based on whatever analytical terms he devised in his mind. For as long as she could remember, Kyle was an over-thinker and was too focused to let someone or something waste too much of his time.

After a little sigh, she said, "Ok dear. That's nice."

Kyle's father was at work that morning and requested, more like ordered, his son to meet him for a late lunch. Kyle had to prepare his mind and attitude before dealing with his father sometimes. His father wasn't exactly condescending, but he had a way of putting words together that could piss someone off if they didn't know him. But this day was different. Kyle was looking forward to the conversation in order to gain a little more insight about military deployments, operations and whatever advice that he may offer. He could bear whatever criticism came his way as long as it was laced with helpful tips and nuggets of knowledge to help his future.

Kyle's father, the retired Colonel, was also an occasional consultant for the military department of a local manufacturing company. This allowed him some flexibility for travel while enjoying his retirement as his leadership experience, organizational expertise, and credentials were put to use as well as deepened the company's profile. In a navy blue suit with a heavily starched white shirt with a lighter blue tie, retired Colonel Scott walked into the Thai restaurant seeking his Lieutenant son. It was engrained in Kyle not to be late when his father asked him to be somewhere. If he arrived late, he would get a lecture about unprofessionalism and tardiness. He heard too many times the speech discussing what the stereotypical tendency for Black people to be late which was known affectionately as "CPT" or "Colored People's Time".

Kyle was sipping on his second glass of water, part of his rehydrating efforts after the bout of drinking the previous night, when they regarded each other. Mr. Scott beamed a very proud smile as he walked over and firmly embraced his son.

"Fuzz," as only his father called him, "what's going on my boy? Your mother pontificated about some woman that you are seeing. It isn't the same one that I met at your class graduation, is it?"

Kyle rolled his eyes when he heard the childhood nickname given to him by his dad, which he assumed his dad didn't see since he kept talking. Kyle really hated that nickname that he earned for spending multiple days and hours grooming the little facial hair that had started to grow while he was in high school.

"You just got in the Army. You still have a little time to bust them in the head before you get married, son."

The 'bust them in the head' statement was his dad's way of saying that he could still have a little fun without commitment. It was probably safe to assume that his father enjoyed being a young, single officer before he settled down with Kyle's mother.

Once, Mr. Scott realized that his son wasn't going to comment, he moved the conversation forward. "It's good that you ran into Lamari and Greg. Did they tell you how the local alumni chapter of brothers here don't want to do any work? They only want to party." Kyle chuckled as he pictured his dad in one of the local fraternity chapter meetings giving the gathered group of men unwanted military operational and tactical guidance as he discussed applying it to service projects and other chapter business.

Mr. Scott continued, "It's good that you are all still friends. I hope it stays that way. You know that they say that you can never go back home. The ones that you call your friends may look at you with disdain and jealousy of your current and future achievements. That is when home will never feel the same to you. Trust me."

Kyle's commented, "I hear you, pops." He had already experienced a little hesitation from some of his high school buddies that chose paths other than college. He couldn't necessarily attribute the awkwardness to jealousy, but he felt that distance and time may have contributed.

"How are your old college roommates doing? Is Rodney enrolled back in school yet?" Kyle's father became quite fond of Jasper and Rodney over the past years when they were roommates. He considered them like sons which he bragged about a little less than his own.

"Jasper is doing great and is better after what happened to him. He still seems a little bitter though. Rodney is not back in school yet, but he is going back once his wife graduates in the spring."

The conversation continued about various subjects as they enjoyed their lunch. Mr. Scott fought the urge to talk about the military just as his son fought the urge to ask. Kyle desperately wanted to ask his father if he ever felt scared and nervous before his deployments, but he couldn't find the words that wouldn't make him seem too petrified. Kyle's mom often commented that he was a shorter version of his dad, including being just as stubborn and prideful.

Kyle had a few more days before it was time to report to his unit. He was enjoying being able to sleep in, work out, and hang out with his friends in the meantime. He was relaxing in preparation for the exciting and challenging world that he was about to enter once he joined up with his Army unit. He hung out with his mom and Mia often, and had short visits with other acquaintances. He drove past his old high school and visited some of his former hangout spots. The unknowns about deploying gave him a desire to reconnect with his surroundings to reminisce about the joys and pains that defined his being.

He wasn't afraid of death, but acknowledged it as a possibility in a war-torn environment. The thought of death brought some things in perspective. He gained a new respect for his father. His father never showed sadness about being away from his family or fear before each deployment to possibly harsh living conditions. He gained a new respect for his mother who stayed strong while the first and only man she ever loved was ordered to leave his family multiple times. She had no guarantees that her husband would return with a sound mind and able body or if he would even return at all.

Kyle decided it best to spend his last night at home with his parents before making the four hour drive to Fort Stewart despite requests from Mia, his frat brothers, Briana, and others. They chose to have dinner at an upscale seafood restaurant that his father frequented. Small talk ensued during dinner with his mother saying the least. She was obviously uneasy about Kyle's future deployment though it may be months from now. The patriarch of the family picked up on her anxiety and the nervousness that his son silently displayed.

After a few failed attempts to garner some laughter, the usual stoic-faced retiree coughed a couple times and drastically changed the conversation to the subject everyone was avoiding.

"Son, you know, ummm … I felt two things when you told me that you enrolled in your school's ROTC program. Pride and fear." He choked up a little before continuing. "I was proud that you were following in your old man's footsteps, but …,"

Those who knew Kyle felt that his hard exterior was partially because of the lack of affection he received from his dad. He always taught Kyle to be tougher and better than everyone around him and that whatever he chose to do, to be the best at it. His father pushed and pushed him in many aspects, but Kyle understood that was his father's way of expressing his love. It was shocking to see his dad choked up … so shocking that he couldn't even look him in the eyes.

Mr. Scott looked at his son with a strong, yet vulnerable reverence as he gripped his wife's hand while she wiped her eyes with a dinner napkin.

"I was proud, but I really hoped that you would have chosen another path." He coughed one last time so he could continue without the crackle in his voice. "You see, it wasn't because I didn't think that you could make it. Hell, you are a Scott man. It was because I didn't want you to go through some of the bullshit and fights that I had to as a black officer in the Army."

Kyle smiled and responded, "I will be ok, dad. Trust me." He almost brought up the nightmares again, but the sad, troubled look on his mom's face told him that it wasn't a good time. He wanted to end the conversation, but it was so rare that his father opened up about anything, that he kept quiet.

After a few more minutes of expressive talking, his father made one last statement on the subject. "Don't ever be afraid to call me for help, advice, or if you just want to complain about the assholes that you work with. Now let's order some dessert before I nibble on your mom to satisfy my sweet tooth."

The mood eased to a more cheerful one as Kyle's mom winked at her husband, and Kyle said, "Yuck."

Chapter 3

A few days at home was good for the soul. After a good night's sleep without the nightmares, Kyle woke up early to load his car for the final leg of his trip. His parents were there to see him off with solemn faces and very few words. His mother hugged him multiple times and held back her tears. His father tried to crack a few jokes to lighten the mood and emphasized to his son that he was available to talk about anything - Army or otherwise.

His father felt all of those emotions that Kyle surely was going through…the butterflies, the anticipation, the fear, and more. It didn't help that he compulsively watched the news to get updates about the war since he found out that his son was to be in a unit destined to deploy. The latest reports on the news made the war on terrorism in Iraq look scarier than anticipated because of the staggering numbers of lives lost. Military and national leaders were starting to rethink how the United States should conduct operations in Iraq.

Even though Kyle was just as nervous as his parents, maybe more so, he was eager to arrive to his unit and to officially begin his career. He received text messages from his friends and members of his family wishing him safe travels and good luck. He replied to none as his mind was focused on the next phase of his life.

In addition to Kyle's father, Jasper spent several nights compulsively staring at his television listening to retired Army Generals, political analysts, and newscasters give updates and opinions about what was transpiring in Iraq. He remembered the look in his friend's eyes when they parted ways the morning he headed to Georgia. Kyle was always good at keeping his emotions in check, but to someone as intuitive as Jasper, his eyes told a different story. Several prayers from both Rodney and Jasper included a special part for their former roommate.

Jasper still occasionally saw the female singer in Rodney's band, Sonya. Though their relationship was mostly physical, it helped him to get over the previous summer's fiasco from his ex-girlfriend, Tina.

After getting caught in bed with one of Jasper's fraternity brothers, Tina conspired a plan to win Jasper back. After her plan failed, she chose to get even by having the same guy that she was caught in bed with, and a couple of other guys, fake a robbery attempt. It went terribly wrong, and all parties that rose against Jasper ended up spending time in jail. The experience had both negative and positive effects on his psyche, and he came out of the scenario a changed man forever.

When it came to how Rodney dealt with the news of his buddy's future deployment, it was different from Jasper. When Rodney was asked about it or whenever he was around Kyle, he displayed that toughness that he typically did in most situations. Statements like "You will be aight," and "He can handle that G.I. Joe shit" spewed from his lips. After a few drinks, the idea of Kyle deploying brought up the gloom that he was hiding. Those around his age were too young to understand the happenings of the Gulf War, but the age of technology and television brought the war in Iraq right to you. He would choke up and express how much he would hate it if something ever happened to Kyle. His wife, Katrina, always teased him about the time they shared a bottle of wine and he told her, "Man, they might as well hand me a rifle and sign me up if they hurt my lil homeboy, Kyle, over there. Why the hell did he do that Army shit anyway?" He would deny it each time that she brought it up.

Kyle turned down his radio as he prepared to show his identification card to the soldier before driving through the main gate of Fort Stewart. It was his first time on the base and he was in awe of how different it was compared to Fort Huachuca. Once he retrieved his ID card from the soldier, who was probably the same age as him, he returned the salute given. As he drove onto base, he turned his music up to a respectable volume for an Army base, but loud enough make his speakers rattle. The mediocre lyrics of the remix of "In Decatur" by Ghetto Mafia blended well with the bass enhanced sample of "Can't Hide Love" by Earth, Wind, and Fire. He smiled as he remembered those nights at 1302 Austin Street in Pembrook, Arkansas. He and his roommates would sip the chosen beverage of the night, take turns freestyling while listening to that song in the same short-phrased, stop-and-go style of Ghetto Mafia.

He looked at the map of Fort Stewart that was part of his welcome packet, and he traced the route to where his unit was. He just had to go and see where he was going to be working before he settled down for the day. He wasn't scheduled to report until the next day, but the anticipation kept him driving. He took in the various surroundings and soldiers walking in and out of each building. After a few minutes, he arrived in front of 53rd Field Artillery and sat in the car. He turned off the engine and took a deep breath.

He saw a small formation assemble in preparation for training. Remembering his father's stories, he got excited when he noticed a couple of black officers amongst the Soldiers. He always heard from his father that he was often the only one on a staff, at an event, and even the only one in the room. It was somewhat comforting for Kyle to see other black officers which temporarily squelched his fear of the same fate of his father . . . at least for the moment.

He sat for a few minutes more daydreaming about how he was going to report to his new boss. He wondered how he would be introduced to the unit - in front of a formation, at a meeting, or maybe not at all. As he touched his keys to start the car, his phone rang. He looked down and smirked as he saw the name on the screen. He hadn't heard from Raven in a couple of days, and had mixed feelings of excitement and frustration when he answered the phone.

"Hey there, young lady. How are you?" Without realizing it, Kyle's already deep voice took a deeper, smoother tone as he spoke.

Second Lieutenant Raven Montgomery felt bad about not returning Kyle's phone calls over the past couple of days, but she was busy settling in to her new unit in Fort Hood, Texas. She reported immediately after their graduation and was currently participating in more training as directed by her commander. Her fatigue was authentic and apparent as she replied, "Hey there, handsome."

Kyle, always blunt and to the point, spewed back, "I haven't heard from you in a few days . . . actually a couple of days. I assume that everything is alright."

Raven rolled her eyes and replied, "Some of us have already starting working, but I'm fine though. Thanks for asking. I was trying to let you spend some time with your family."

Kyle felt that he was on the verge of pushing too far and decided not to make his next sarcastic-flavored response. He really liked Raven, but he was not the type to let too many women close to him. Their relationship started off as study partners, then study partners with benefits, but it morphed into something a little more in the last weeks of their Military Intelligence Officer Basic Course at Fort Huachuca. The relationship had gotten to the point where Kyle felt compelled to ask her if she wanted to continue it after the course ended.

They continued the conversation for a few minutes talking about their new bases and work expectations, then ended with a little flirtatious talk and a promise of more after he settled in for the night. Afterwards, he left the unit area and passed the apartment complex where he'd be staying temporarily on his way to grab something to eat. He already had the key mailed to him while he was at his father's house, so he was not worried about signing in until the next day.

After a trip to the nearest Burger King's drive-thru, Kyle pulled up to the Willowcrest Apartments. He grabbed his bags and headed to the furnished unit. His father convinced him not to buy furniture to fill the apartment until his deployment, despite the additional cost each month. He walked in and surveyed every room and appliance before sitting to eat. He breathed a sigh of relief then said his grace.

The excitement of the day was waning, and a feeling of lonesomeness crept in. After unpacking and watching some TV, he called Jasper just to talk to someone familiar. He needed some jokes and positive vibes at the moment.

Jasper was at home playing video games when he answered the phone. "Wassup homeboy? You all ready to save the world and shit?"

Kyle felt compelled to be honest again though he didn't want to dampen the mood of the conversation. "No, I'm not ready. I . . . uh . . . got a question." He took a deep breath, "Uh . . . how did you get ready for your first day of work? Did you go to bed early, have a drink, or something?"

Jasper felt that Kyle was overreacting as usual, but he knew the feeling. He was a nervous wreck the night before starting his job at InfoTech Solutions. Kyle continued with his thought-up scenarios of "what-ifs" and "should-I" questions. Jasper finally interrupted him and said, "Look bruh, you are going to be fine. You always do the damn thing in everything you do. You will be straight. Do some pushups, eat dinner, and iron your clothes. If that doesn't work, jack off and go to bed."

Kyle felt that he would be ok, but he just needed to hear it. Jasper was always a sounding board to Kyle as well as Rodney. Jasper just had a way of listening and understanding regardless of who was talking to him. After a few more minutes of conversation, a couple of more "what-ifs", and some of Jasper's comedic responses, Kyle felt a little bit better. "Thanks man" were his final words before ending the call. Now feeling better, he called Raven before going to bed.

The day began early for Kyle as he polished his boots again and had a quick workout in his apartment. After a shower, he pulled out his dry cleaned, heavily starched battle dress uniform. He didn't have to sign in until 10 a.m., but he rushed anyway. Not knowing how good or bad the traffic was going to be on the way to the base made him nervous.

He left his apartment and walked over to the leasing office to sign his lease. The process was fairly painless which helped dab some of his anxiety of the day. After signing his paperwork, he hopped in the car, said a quick prayer, and started his trek toward Fort Stewart. It didn't take him long to make it to the gate of the base that was closest to his unit, the 53rd Field Artillery Battalion.

The blast of cool autumn air that greeted him when he opened the door removed his edginess and made him wish that he placed his black fleece jacket in the car. The day at the unit had already begun so there was no formation on the grass next to the battalion's building. No Soldiers were there to greet him or were around for him to ask for directions. Kyle decided to walk into the back door that he saw some guy walk out of the day prior.

Feeling like an outsider, he stepped in what looked like a conference room of some sort. There was no one there at the time, which was a relief for Kyle. He looked around and saw pictures of the commander, his new boss, and some of the staff. He counted only one other black officer on the primary staff. He shrugged, for he wasn't shocked because of his father's stories.

He walked out the main entrance of the room which led to a hallway full of offices. He passed a vending machine and then saw the staff duty desk. A young Sergeant was sitting there watching a small TV.

Kyle approached the desk which made the young Sergeant pop up. "Sir, how may I help you?" Kyle said, "Good morning, I am Lieutenant Kyle Scott, and I am here to report and sign in."

"The Soldier replied, "Roger, sir. Sign this book right here, and I will call the S1." The S1 was the staff proponent of the unit that handled personnel related actions. As soon as Kyle finished signing in, a powerful, booming voice called out his name.

"Kyle Scott? Hey there, Lieutenant! Welcome to the 53rd." Kyle recognized the name on the chest of the uniform of the man approaching. Like a hardened warrior who sounded like a fast talking car salesman, Lieutenant Colonel Bloomberg walked toward Kyle and gave him a firm handshake while looking in his eyes. One of the first childhood lessons that Kyle's dad taught him was to always look someone in the eyes, even when intimidated.

Applicable at the moment, Kyle returned the look to his commander, and said, "Sir, it is nice to be here and finally meet you. I am ready to get started."

After a hefty laugh, the Commander said, "I am sure you are, Kyle. Take care of your in-processing first; there is plenty of work for you to do when you finish up. I spoke to your dad earlier. He called two hours ago to check on your arrival. You sound just like him." Kyle stifled a frown upon hearing that. The commander began walking away and turned back toward the Sergeant at the desk and said, "Sergeant Wilson, did you call the S1? Let's get the L-T taken care of."

Halfway down the hallway, the Commander turned back around and boomed, "Kyle, welcome to the team! I have a conference call in a few minutes, but I will check on you later. HOOAH!" Afterward, Kyle was greeted by another noncommissioned officer, Staff Sergeant Mark Jefferson, who took him through the drill of filling out various forms before sending him to the central in-processing hub for all incoming personnel. While he was completing the paperwork, his boss, Captain Michael Cueva, walked in the S1 office to introduce himself. He told Kyle that he was going to be assigned as the Human Intelligence Officer and the Assistant S2. The S2 position handles all of the intelligence requirements for the battalion, whether friendly or enemy.

The rest of the day was fairly uneventful and were followed by days of briefings and more paperwork. Captain Cueva sent him a text message stating that he should enjoy the rest of the week after his in-processing and not to worry about coming back to the office until Monday. Kyle was glad to hear it and planned on using the time to explore the area. Something his dad said became his plan of action as he would begin exploring the area . . . find a good barber, a good soul food restaurant, and the mall.

Monday morning, Lieutenant Scott arrived to formation with the Soldiers from his unit for physical training. Not knowing anyone or where he should stand, he stood in the back trying not to appear lost. He remained in the rear of the battalion as they formed four smaller formations. He fought the urge to walk back to his car and just return later. He did not see the battalion commander or his boss.

The Chaplain of the 53rd Field Artillery Battalion saw how confused Kyle appeared as he floundered in an attempt to get in where he would fit. The Chaplain's job, and his personality, was to welcome all those who were new and be available to those who simply needed to talk. He walked over to Kyle and offered his hand. Kyle smiled when he recognized him as the only other black officer from the staff photo in the conference room.

Captain Chaplain Elliot Mosley smiled genuinely, shook Kyle's hand, and introduced himself. "You must be the new L-T. We form up over here. You can come stand by me, and I will introduce you to some of the other staff."

Chaplain Mosley was an older man with a flawlessly shaved head and thin glasses. To Kyle, he sounded like some of his uncles and guys that he grew up around as a young Georgia boy – strong with a strong southern accent to match. Judging from his voice alone, he could have either been a pastor or a pimp. The contradiction made him smile. He was glad that the Chaplain saved him from possible embarrassment. "Thanks, sir. I already heard too many jokes about Lieutenants being lost, and today was not the day for that."

Chaplain Mosley smiled again and said, "I got you, young brother. Welcome to the unit." He then proceeded to introduce him to a few of the staff members and some of the nearby Soldiers before the Command Sergeant Major of the unit walked out of the door. Kyle noticed that his boss, CPT Cueva, didn't really speak or acknowledge anyone when he walked up.

Command Sergeant Major Kenneth Tucker was the highest ranking enlisted soldier in the unit and looked just as hardened as the unit's commander. His speedy, yet intense walk made all of the formations tighten up and get ready for the order of "Fall in!!" With that order, the physical training, or PT, session began. Chaplain Mosley pulled Kyle aside to ask if he wanted to go to the gym with him since he didn't run much while recovering from a previous ankle injury. Kyle agreed, and they took the opportunity to talk as they walked to the gym.

The two black officers talked about the unit, their relationships, church, and a myriad of subjects as they lifted weights. Kyle was shocked at how much weight the older gentleman could bench press and lift for his bicep curls. Hanging out with Captain Mosley was a nice welcome to the unit and Kyle's anxieties calmed for a while. He was hoping that the nightmares he had would stop now that he made it to his unit.

Chapter 4

The stress of managing the band, "Dipped in Soul", working another job part-time, and playing at one of the churches in Pembrook, had been wearing Rodney down for some time. He often daydreamed about how life would have been if his wife, Katrina, didn't get pregnant before his senior year of college. He wasn't angry with her – he loved being married to such a supportive woman. Every time his thoughts got the best of him, he would think about the blessing of his daughter, Ayana. She was the motivation to keep going whenever his muscles ached or he could have used some more sleep. Also, he made a promise to his wife that she should finish school and take care of the house, while he made the ends meet.

Katrina nagged him about taking it easy, but she knew his soul yearned to play music. All of his conflicts, his greatness, and his desires were woven into the chords and scales that he played on his bass guitar. She supported her husband without question and felt that their financial strain was temporary. His sacrifices motivated her to finish school as fast as she could. She wanted to lighten his burden and do her part to build for their future.

That particular day, she walked in on him while he was asleep in the living room. Sheet music was scattered across the coffee table while their daughter napped on his stomach. She silently said a quick prayer of thanks for a beautiful family with a great man to lead it.

Kyle's first couple of weeks at Fort Stewart were filled with orientation tasks and staff meetings as his unit prepared to conduct field training exercises before deployment. The staff and leadership welcomed him. The Soldiers in his staff section and in the unit were also receptive.

He had a couple of minor incidents that pushed his comfort level a little, but his father's stories prepared him on how to react. The first incident occurred after the last duty formation one Thursday. The wife of the executive officer of the unit, Major Pandor, was standing in the parking lot waiting for him. She noticed Kyle walking to his car and approached him to ask if he had seen her husband. Kyle explained to her that Major Pandor was called by the unit's commander to huddle for a quick meeting with some of the staff. The Caucasian woman thanked Kyle, introduced herself, and stated, "LT Scott, welcome to Fort Stewart. You speak so well. Where did you go to school?"

Although he was shocked and seething with disgust about her comment, he simply replied with, "Well, thank you for welcoming me to Fort Stewart, ma'am. I went to Pembrook College which is affectionately called the Black West Point due to the outstanding officers that we produce."

Once in the car, he said to himself, "What the fuck does she mean 'you speak so well'?" Kyle always spoke with less of a twang than his peers who were originally from the south, whether black or white, and he was offended by the comment.

The following Tuesday, he was returning from lunch and walked past a small group of enlisted Soldiers taking a smoke break near the unit's headquarters building. Three were black, one was white, and two of them were around Kyle's age. The oldest one was the senior noncommissioned officer, or NCO, of the intelligence staff section, Sergeant First Class Tobias Johnson.

One of the other Soldiers, Sergeant Willis, jokingly made a comment to Kyle, "When are you going to get a new car, sir? You a LT, so you need to gone get one. "

Kyle had noticed that some of the Soldiers had better cars than him at such a young age. He assumed they were spending their enlistment bonus money on their cars rather than investing or saving for the future. Kyle was more conscious of savings and investments and replied, "I don't know. I'm not really worried about it right now. Maybe when we return from the deployment."

Sergeant Willis replied too casually to address an officer. "Shiiit, sir. You need to do that if you want to get any ass around here. These hoes be jocking fly rims and shit here. You ain't going to get it with that car. You might be too dark-skinned anyway. The hoes around here like the slim, light-skinned pimps, like me."

The others in the group laughed, but stopped once they saw that Lieutenant Scott wasn't. Kyle used to have difficulty giving orders to Soldiers that were older but lower in rank than he. His southern home training taught him to always respect his elders, and he subconsciously did so without thinking at times. But after Sergeant Willis's remark, that difficulty fleeted as he stated, "Sergeant First Class Johnson, as a senior NCO, I can't believe you just allowed such bullshit to be spoken to me and in front of the battalion headquarters. You laughing right along with them when you know better. He focused back on the one cracking on him and said, "Fuck that...Sergeant Willis, you know better. "

The group instantly straightened up upon hearing the serious tone of Kyle's deep voice getting louder. "Not only did you talk such foolishness . . . rims, hoes, skin color, and shit . . . you said that nonsense with people walking by and in front of people not of our race." He looked at Specialist Woods, the only Caucasian in the group, and said, "No offense, Woods." His attention quickly went back to Sergeant Willis and concluded with, "You may not know me and may not like me after this, but I don't give a fuck. What you *will* do is respect my rank and respect yourself as a Soldier, a man, and a black man around here. I would tell you to drop and give me some pushups, but I think Sergeant First Class Johnson knows what to do."

With that last statement, Kyle walked off, disturbed by what he heard and surprised that that words he had just spoken came out of his mouth. His father always told him that some Soldiers will try you until you prove them wrong. He also told his son that unfortunately, it would probably be the Black Soldiers who would do the trying.

Weeks later, the Soldiers of 53rd Field Artillery Battalion returned from a week long exercise right before the Thanksgiving holiday break. It involved test scenarios to validate some the unit's training for the upcoming deployment. Kyle was bored while in the field, (or designated outside training area) since his staff section didn't have much to do. He spent a lot of his time reading and talking with members of the unit.

His girlfriend Raven was coming to visit and spend Thanksgiving with him. She was scheduled to arrive around 10 p.m. on Wednesday. Kyle had already planned to cook a large meal of his favorite soul food. He decided against going home or to Jasper's parents' house like he used to do in college. He had local offers that he declined as well, including an invitation from Chaplain Mosley. He didn't want to bother another Soldier and their family and be deemed as some lonely soul with nowhere to go.

When Raven arrived, he fought to keep his excitement down, both on his face and in his pants. He casually gave her a hug while getting her luggage in his attempt to play it cool. Once they got to his apartment, he no longer fought his craving. Meticulous about hygiene, he offered her some towels as soon as they opened the door. Raven was longing for affection just as much as Kyle and knew the routine. She rushed to the bathroom and washed up after her flight.

She walked out naked, just how Kyle preferred, and was greeted by a naked Kyle. No longer playing it cool, he grabbed her and said, "Looks like you have been doing a lot of extra physical training."

She regarded his body and replied, "Looks like you have been hitting some extra PT as well."

In typical Kyle fashioned, he smirked and just said, "Yeah."

They groped and rubbed each other in the middle of the living room for a few minutes. As their heartbeats sped up and moaning followed, Raven pushed him back and grabbed a condom from her purse. Kyle was sitting on the couch waiting. With a devilish look in his eyes and a smirk, he bluntly asked, "So, umm . . . would you mind doing a little something for me?" He looked down at his penis and then into Raven's eyes completely serious about his request. Without any reservation or hesitation, she rushed over and proceed to fulfill what he wanted.

As she willfully complied, Kyle thought about how Jasper used to marvel at how easily he could just ask for some head without fumbling his words or just dropping hints whereas most guys wouldn't be so bold. Kyle would always tell him, *"A closed mouth doesn't get fed. If you want it, you ask for that shit. The worst she can say is no."*

After of couple of rounds of passionate and aggressive intercourse, they both cleaned themselves up and proceeded to start preparing Thanksgiving dinner. Kyle turned on his stereo and played a compilation CD with various booty shake music on it including songs by 95 South and the Ying Yang Twins.

It was the beginning of a wonderful weekend full of passionate lovemaking, conversations about life and the Army, and time to solidify their relationship. They were both scared about Kyle's upcoming deployment, but they enjoyed the moments they were together during the holiday.

Chapter 5

LTC Bloomberg promised that the men and women of 53rd Field Artillery would not deploy before January 1st of 2004. Whether it was for morale or Department of Army planning, all were happy to spend the holidays with their loved ones and friends. Most already knew their approximate deployment date that would start with different elements of the staff departing at different times. Due to the intelligence gathering and planning that Kyle and his staff section had to do, he was going to be one of the first to take the long flight into foreign lands of uncertainty. His orders said January 15th, but it could've been a week before or after that date.

In late December, operations at the unit were pretty much slow to allow Soldiers to handle any last minute arrangements, pack for the deployment, and to spend as much time with their families as possible. Packing lists were distributed, power of attorney documents were signed, and the military vehicles and weapons were cleaned and ready for shipping.

Chaplain Mosley was busy counseling Soldiers and spouses collectively and individually. With all that was portrayed in the news reports concerning the war, it was expected for them to be nervous. War made anyone nervous, especially the troops that were partaking in their first one.

Kyle's nightmares were befalling almost every night. Beheadings, erroneous intelligence assessments disappointment from his unit and parents all troubled him every time that he closed his eyes for the night. Sleep was hard to come by on most days until he passed out from lack of it. He finally told Raven about the nightmares. Her words sometimes brought temporary solace as they prayed together or she simply said, "All will be ok. Trust me."

Even Jasper and Rodney were growing more anxious as the days before Kyle's deployment grew shorter and shorter. Rodney was in denial and chose not to talk about it, but Jasper stayed glued to his television watching CNN and other news channels. The number of Servicemember deaths were growing daily, and the mini memorials of the fallen that CNN showed before each commercial break troubled Jasper the most. He wanted to believe that his homeboy was coming back to the United States in good mind, body, and spirit. Military combat had a way of sometimes breaking the strongest of wills . . . even people as mentally tough as Kyle.

Kyle's parents drove down to Savannah on January 13th to spend some time with him before his departure and close out his apartment for him after he left. Mr. Scott rummaged through his bags and trunks to ensure that he had everything that he felt his son needed. Ms. Scott cooked almost anything that her son wanted. Kyle was just appreciative that his parents were able to stop their normal lives to see him off. Raven didn't have enough leave days saved up and couldn't make the trip which Kyle understood.

It was possible that Kyle's departure was going to get pushed to a later date, but he had to check in daily for updates. In the meantime, Kyle enjoyed the time with his parents and received plenty of phone calls from his friends. One particular phone call troubled him.

Mia called later that afternoon and was crying hysterically. "Kyle, tell them you can't go! If something . . . if anything . . . oh my god!" Kyle tried to calm her down during the breaks of her sobbing. "Why does the President have to fight this damn war, Kyle? I don't understand."

Kyle remained calm as it was his duty to serve. The events of September 11, 2001 instilled a new sense of patriotism in many Americans, including him. He, like most Soldiers, just wanted to do their part to fight and end the war on terrorism. As he spoke to Mia that night, he wondered if the war was justified. It wasn't up to him to question the sense of the war, he was given his orders and that was the end of it. History would one day reveal if it was all worth it.

Probably spurred by Mia's conversation, Kyle had another nightmare while he napped for a couple of hours. It was unusual for him to have them any other time than at night. The Scott's were hanging out at Kyle's apartment drinking coffee and having small talk while he slept. Highly attentive due to his years of military service, Mr. Scott thought that he heard grumbling between some of Kyle's snoring. He looked in on his son and saw him squirm a bit. He thought nothing of it as he closed the door.

It wasn't until he overheard Kyle tell Raven about the nightmares that he chose to ask. After the conversation ended, Kyle stepped out of his room and saw his dad drinking another cup of coffee while he stared at him. With a look of intensity, Mr. Scott whispered, "Fuzz, let's take a ride. Just you and I. Let's keep your mom out of this." Not sure of what was going on, Kyle just shook his head in agreement. "Hey lil sexy, me and Fuzz are going to run to the liquor store down the street. You need anything?" She was oblivious to the true reason for the ride and simply shook her head no.

In the car, the two Scott men rode in silence for a couple of minutes. To break it, Kyle joked about how he wish he could get a piece of his girlfriend before he hopped on that plane. Reginald Scott looked at his son, smiled to keep the mood light, and said, "It is always nice to get some ol' 'bust em in the head' before a deployment. Since you can't, you better get ready to start jacking off."

After some laughter from both of them, the elder Scott man became serious again and continued, "I wasn't really listening, but I did hear you say something about recurring nightmares. What's going on, Fuzz?" Kyle dropped his head and looked out of the passenger side window. "Yeah, I overheard you getting your phone pimping on with your lady. You can tell your dad, man."

Not sure about what he wanted to lie about, Kyle just remained silent. Part of him wanted to just ask his dad questions to gain a veteran's perspective on the nightmares, and a part of him was very mad that it even came up. Either way, he really didn't want to talk about it.

"Son, I asked you a question." Kyle's father was dealing with sudden confliction at the moment too. He wanted to be supportive and assist his son anyway that he could, but part of him was angry that his son never really opened up to him about personal matters. During his military career, he felt the pre-deployment jitters, the urge to review his life's purpose, and the weird acceptance that he may not return from the deployment the same man . . . or even alive. He could relate to his son's nightmares as well. "Son, I said that I asked a question."

Kyle, so much like his dad, often played the stubbornness role until he felt he had to budge. In order to keep the peace, he decided to tell him about the nightmares after some conditions first. He wasn't in the mood to deal with his dad's nagging at the moment. "Aight dad. I will tell you what's up, but I don't need you to do the typical you. No offense, but you know what I mean."

Understanding that his son's mind was filled with bombarding thoughts about the deployment, he kept quiet. The conversation started slowly, but it picked up after they returned to Kyle's car with the bottle of Crown Royal. It was good for Mr. Scott to impart bits of wisdom to his son and relive good and bad moments of a somewhat glorious military career. It was even better for Kyle to hear that he was not weird for having nightmares and random thoughts about warfare.

They laughed, cussed, and told some truths that they both wanted to get off of their chests. Not wanting to shake up the mood and dialogue, they sat in the parking lot passing the bottle of liquor back and forth while they talked. The elder Scott was honestly the more scared of the two. War was different and more conventional during his tenure. The enemies against the United States seemed more menacing and heartless in recent war compared to those of the past. He had for years accepted the possibilities of battle, but the possibility of burying his son due to a war tied up in political agendas and fiscal limitations, troubled him more than he cared to show.

Suddenly, Kyle's cell phone rang. It was his boss calling to let him know that he was on the roster to depart sometime the next day. "Roger, sir! I will be ready to roll tomorrow when it's time," Kyle replied. With the mood abruptly turning to somber, both men got out of the car without saying another word.

Once inside, Ms. Scott could look at the two important men in her life and discern what had occurred. "Baby, let's leave our son to a lil alone time. Tomorrow is a big day." Mr. Scott tried to sound strong as he got those words out without choking and holding back tears.

Regardless, the matriarch was behaving as expected for a mother who was about to see her son off to war. After fifteen minutes or more of tears from his wife, he pulled them both close to him to say a quick prayer. Once again, the father tried to lighten the mood with humor. He told his wife, "Baby, I need you to get it together so we can go back to the hotel. If you are good, I will let you lay that sexy body next to me nude in the king-sized bed in our room."

Shortly after, Kyle's parents left. He decided to talk to Raven for a few minutes before he shaved and took a shower. Then he went over his packing list quickly before putting on his uniform, minus the boots and camo top. He figured that he would get dressed early and sleep in his partial attire as a way to accept that he was a Soldier prepared to make the ultimate sacrifice for his country. He poured himself a final drink of Crown Royal liquor and sat in the armchair in the corner of his living room. Calmness and acceptance crept in while his buzz from the brown liquor increased. He hoped to doze off in that chair with his mind at peace and without the nightmares. There was a little bit of liquor left in his glass. His last thought before nodding off was returning home from the war.

Chapter 6

Kyle arrived to his unit's holding area with the next group of Soldiers who were leaving for war in a foreign land at around 9 a.m. His parents picked up breakfast at one of the local fast food spots and met him at the pre-staging area around eight. His mom held herself together better that day compared to the previous night. Perhaps, she had a moment of acceptance as well. Kyle wasn't sure.

While they sat in one of Fort Stewart's gymnasiums and ate, they partook in positive dialogue . . . no one wanted to change the mood. Other families were doing similar activities including Soldiers playing cards with their children or spouses just holding each other in silence. The officer in charge of moving the deploying Soldiers announced that the flight had been delayed for several hours. They were to stay in the vicinity and await further instructions. Everyone seemed relieved to hear that they had more time to be with their loved ones.

Eventually, Kyle decided to give his mom an envelope containing his unit's forwarding address in Iraq and contact information of the spouses in the unit's family readiness group along with the will and power of attorney. She couldn't bring herself to accept the envelope so her husband took it and changed the subject.

"Have you spoken to your homeboys yet?" Kyle's dad noticed how often his son's cell phone buzzed with text messages. "What about Raven? I know you spoke to her." Kyle sat there indifferently, not revealing either nervousness, sadness, or excitement. "Kyle, why don't you step away and call your friends? We'll be here."

Still silent, Kyle stood up and flipped open his cell phone. As he dialed Lamari's number, he saw his parents embrace each other out of the corner of his eye because his mother couldn't keep up the strong front she had all morning. Hearing her loud sigh, followed by Mr. Scott telling her to keep it together for Kyle, almost made his knees buckle. As Kyle felt himself about to lose it, Lamari answered the phone call.

"What's up, lil dude? How you feel? You ready?" Kyle didn't respond immediately. Lamari knew his friend's silence meant that he was holding in his real thoughts. "Bruh, you got this shit! We are all about achieving and striving to rise above adversity. Pledging taught us that. You got this."

Kyle laughed and stated, "You are right. I got this. Yo, did Greg ever holla at Mia?" Wild laughter erupted in the phone coming from Lamari. "Hell no, she ain't trying to hear that from Greg. He'll probably try a few times before you get back."

The frat brothers talked for a few minutes before ending the call. Kyle called Greg next, but there was no answer. He called some of his family and spoke to them for a few minutes each. One of his uncles asked if they could pray before hanging up. The phone call to Mia was next.

Mia answered already sounding like she had been crying. Her first words were, "Is your lady friend there with you to say bye?" Upon hearing that she wasn't, she said under her breath, "I still don't like the bitch."

When Kyle didn't respond as he typically would, she continued, "Soldier boy, you ready to do this?" It sounded like she was trying to hold back more tears as she talked in her typical loud, accent-filled voice. "I wish you would've came to see me again before you left. I would have sent you off right . . . shiiit. Would have gave your ass something to dream about and shit."

Kyle jumped in, "Now, Mia, you know…"

Mia jumped back in and cut him off with, "I know… I know. You got a girl and stuff. I still don't like the bitch even though I ain't met her." She didn't mumble when she said the bitch comment for the second time.

They continued for a few minutes more, and Mia promised to throw Kyle a big party when he got back to the United States. She carried on about various topics and kept him laughing the whole time. Kyle needed the comedy that Mia spewed right then, but decided to cut the conversation off before she got too emotional. He realized that his female best friend knew him probably better than anyone and may even be in love with him.

"Mia, I need to call Jasper before they tell us to go. I promise to email you when I get a chance. Ok?" While wiping a tear from her eye, she replied, "Ok", before hanging up. Jasper was next on his call list.

After brief conversations with Jasper and Jasper's father, Kyle made the phone call that he was most dreading. Rodney answered on the first ring, "About time you called me back muthfucka! Had me all worried and shit." Rodney, big in stature and physically intimidating to some, was the most emotional of Kyle's male friends. He talked tough for a few more statements, then his voice cracked. "Nigga, you be careful over there. You hear me!" From voice cracking to full out crying, Rodney continued talking not giving Kyle a chance to respond. "I mean….dude, don't let those muthafuckas over there . . . get you. Be careful."

During their phone call, Kyle had walked outside and around the corner of the gym. Finally alone and replaying the words of his friends and family, he became overcome with emotion. Hearing Rodney crying took him over the edge. As Rodney got himself together, tears streamed down Kyle's face as he said, "Playa, I will be ok. I'm a little bit scared, but I got this. Don't worry about me, big dawg. Hello…?"

Kyle's words were met with silence. After a few seconds, he heard, "Hey Kyle, this is Katrina. Rodney had to walk away from the phone. I will tell him what you said."

Rodney's wife, Katrina, picked up the phone as her husband walked away. Kyle could hear him in the background though saying, "Lord, please look over my lil homie. Please!"

He could only say to Katrina in response, "Ok." Then she started to cry herself as she said, "We are praying for you, Kyle. Come on back home, and I will cook you and Rodney a big meal. Ok? Ok?"

Kyle wiped another tear and responded with, "Ok. I will talk to you guys later." He hung up the phone and took a deep breath. He promised himself that he wasn't going to cry anymore and dried his eyes before walking back into the gym.

Minutes later, the buses taking them to the departure point were parked outside of the gym. Even though the deploying soldiers were not leaving at the moment, the atmosphere inside became more solemn. The officer in charge announced, "Everyone, let me get your attention. We will start loading the buses in an hour to head toward the plane. There are some sandwiches and meals still available thanks to the volunteers from the Fort Stewart Military Wives association." Many soldiers grabbed extra meals and snacks in preparation for travel for an unknown amount of time.

Spouses grabbed their loved ones a little tighter and crying was heard throughout the gym while Soldiers consoled their families. Some of the Soldiers who were not deploying, came to hang out with their buddies that were departing. It was heartbreaking and awe-inspiring at the same time to see the love and support.

Kyle saw that Raven was calling him, but he wasn't ready to talk to her yet. He wanted to save that phone call when he arrived at the airplane boarding site. He sat next to his parents and engaged in random talk and jokes. He was glad to see his mom smiling and his dad laying off of the military jargon and advice.

Kyle told his dad during the conversation, "You know what I want when I get back, right? I want a bottle of Crown Royal and some chicken wings in your hands when I get off the plane."

In his typical smart aleck fashion, his dad replied, "You better send some of that tax-free money before you place your order, little Lieutenant." The three of them laughed and continued to converse until it was time to leave.

One of the local government officials approached the microphone that was on a small decorated stage in the gym and introduced herself before thanking the Soldiers and their families for "serving our great nation unselfishly". An uneasy feeling was in Kyle's stomach because it meant that it was time to start loading the buses and saying goodbyes. She was followed by the Commanding General of Fort Stewart who gave a similar message, but it was more motivational and rehearsed. A chaplain from one of the local units led a quick prayer after the General's remarks. The final speaker to hit the stage was the officer in charge who told everyone to get ready to leave in five minutes.

A flurry of emotions could be seen amongst the crowd of Soldiers and supporters in the gym. The officer in charge, who was sympathetic to those who were about to deploy, still had a job to do and called the troops to fall in formation. The time to say goodbye was over, and the move toward Iraq was officially beginning. The Fort Stewart Band Detachment starting playing a festive march as the soldiers were instructed to walk to the buses. Cameras flashed, and families waved signs and cheered.

The bus ride to the airplanes was only 20 minutes. As some of the Soldiers chatted excitedly, Kyle just looked out of the window, lost in his thoughts. He thought about his mother's face, and his dad's words. He thought about rubbing and kissing on Raven and taking a sip of Crown Royal. He thought about Taco Bell food and all of the television shows that he would miss while away. When they arrived, the officer in charge hopped on each bus and made some administrative announcements including leave times, locations of restrooms in the hangar and other minor information.

Large contracted airplanes awaited them as they filed off of the bus. Some of the junior enlisted Soldiers were pulled away to be part of a work detail that loaded the duffle bags and other gear on large pallets. Kyle sat in a corner and flipped open his phone. There were texts from some of his friends and one from his mom that simply stated, "I love you." He called Raven who answered on the first ring.

"Hey baby!! I was waiting on your call. I figured that you had left already." Kyle smiled at the genuine excitement in her voice. He appreciated her ability to always bring a smile to his face. They were opposites in as many ways as they were the same. He liked how she always cracked a joke when he was being long-winded in about something he saw on television. He felt silly and free when they were together, despite being in a world where his seriousness and urgent nature was necessary just to be considered good enough.

"Hey there, lil lady. I wanted to call you last so we could talk as long as needed . . . or until my cell phone battery dies." They talked about war expectations, his nightmares, and previous conversations with his friends, and their relationship status.

"Listen there, Raven, I understand if you want to just chill until I get back. Really, I would understand." Kyle said it so matter-of-factly that it bothered her tremendously.

"Kyle, what are you afraid of? I don't call too many guys my boyfriend, so this ain't a game to me," Raven said in utter shock.

"I mean, it may be hard not to have someone there like that for you." Kyle meant well, but it wasn't what Raven wanted to hear. Maybe the deployment had his head foggy, and he was scared that he would need Raven more than she understood.

The officer in charge of the flight ran into the hangar and stated, "Ok folks! Let's grab your gear, use the bathroom one last time, and get ready to roll!" He ran out just as fast as he came in on his way to perhaps handle final details before boarding.

Kyle felt compelled to continue to make his point to Raven, but the statement of the officer in charge shook him out of it. "Baby, I just want you to be there for me. I . . . um . . . care about you . . . a lot. I mean, I . . . shit . . . really like you, and I don't want . . ."

Raven jumped in and stated, "Listen, Lieutenant Scott, I like you too, so stop fucking tripping. I ain't going to fuck anybody or be fucking with anybody. Stop that shit now, and get your mind right before you get on the plane." Kyle understood and had to fight the urge to finish his earlier point.

To change the tone to one of happier spirits, Kyle said, "Ok. I got ya. Cool. So Raven, I may not be able to say something back to you with all these people around, but I want you to tell me what we would have done if you were in my apartment last night." He let go of all of the anxiety as Raven proceeded to tell the freaky details of what would have been a fun night if she was actually there.

It wasn't quite love yet that he felt, but the feeling of whatever they had was growing. It felt right when he asked her to be his girlfriend. He didn't overanalyze it like usual when he made that decision. He really wished that he could have felt her body next to his before he got on that plane.

Fifteen minutes later, Kyle and the other deploying Soldiers were making their way to the airplane whose final destination was Kuwait. The Commanding General of Fort Stewart was at the end of a red carpet that led to the plane and shook each person's hand. As Kyle climbed the steps, he looked over his left shoulder and saw families standing outside the gated area still waving signs and cheering. He assumed his parents were on the road back to Alpharetta. He was ready for what was to be once he got off the plane on the other side. Actually, he was already looking forward to coming back.

Chapter 7

Jasper was leaving Shelia's downtown apartment when his phone rang. Shelia was his supervisor at InfoTech Solutions where he was a helpdesk representative. He went over to her place occasionally to continue their secret sexual relationship. When he tried to pull away, due to the risk of getting caught and the weirdness of it all, Shelia started showering Jasper with gifts to keep him coming around. As much as he enjoyed the sex and the gifts, he knew Shelia wasn't the one for him.

He grunted when he saw the name on his phone; it was one of his other sexual exploits, nicknamed "Pretty Titty Vivian". She had been blowing his phone up lately for a follow-up to their previous freaky encounter some time ago. He just looked at the phone while it rang on his seat until it went to voicemail. He had too many ladies on his plate, and he really didn't want to deal with one that was begging and pleading for more attention. Jasper thought to himself, "*I ain't got time. I ain't got time.*"

On the way home, he thought about writing Kyle a letter to talk about his dating situation. Not that he didn't want to write a letter asking about his war experience thus far, but he figured that enough people were writing him asking those type of questions. He missed being able to pick up the phone and vent to his friend because he knew that he was going to get advice that made sense. Kyle was always the rational one out of the three Men of 1302, and Jasper could have really talked to him at the time.

Even if Jasper had written the letter with a forwarding address to the operating base in Iraq, Kyle wouldn't have received for weeks. Kyle was in Kuwait at a temporary base that served as a staging area as more soldiers, vehicles, and equipment were arriving into the theater of war. Tall barriers enclosed a series of large, heavy duty tents with built in wood structures to form offices. Multiple towers were situated around the base for lookouts, and multiple patrols of Soldiers traveled around the base constantly.

He spent most of his days in intelligence synchronization meetings with his staff and with soldiers in his particular section. He focused mainly on planning the upcoming convoy that parts of his unit would travel to get to where they would be stationed for at least a year.

Though Kyle was busier than most of the Soldiers that had already arrived from his unit, he had a lot of downtime. He spent it in the gym constructed in the morale, welfare, and recreation (known as MWR) tents. The other side was filled with magazines, video games, and air conditioned seating areas. Chaplain Mosley arrived a few days after Kyle and would join him in the gym for at least one of the twice-a-day sessions he partook in to pass the time.

There was a large mobile shelter, owned by AT&T that was built near one of the big tents. The shelter allowed Soldiers to make phone calls back home after purchasing calling cards with preset amounts of minutes. He called his parents a couple of times to let them know that he had arrived safely, but he waited in the long lines almost daily just to talk to Raven for a few moments to talk about what was happening.

Among the subjects he discussed with his girlfriend, he told her more about his nightmares that he still had almost every night. Even though he would toss and turn in his sleep every night in the tent where several Soldiers slept, no one thought anything of it. The cots that they slept on were not the most comfortable, so everyone tossed and turned a bit. Kyle was just glad that he never cried out in his sleep during one of his episodes for that would have been embarrassing.

He enjoyed her voice telling him that it would be ok before talking about the erotic things they would do when he returned, and it kept him sane – more than she realized. Kyle was glad that he decided to ask Raven to be his girl. She had proven to be a valued pillar of support during the beginning of his trying times.

One particular time that they were talking, Raven named songs they could put on a CD to serve as a playlist for their reunion. He also suggested artists like Marvin Gaye, Teddy Pendergrass, and the Whispers. It was obvious that he was influenced by his father's taste in music while she wanted something more current like Al. B. Sure and H-Town. As they laughed about it, the phone call suddenly ended. The remaining minutes expired on his phone card. He was so into the conversation that he forgot that he didn't have much time left. Mad at his own oversight, he whispered, "Damn", as he hung up.

Kyle walked out into the warm, dark Kuwaiti night filled with sounds of the generators running in various places that provide electricity to the temporary structures and lights scattered around the base. Though the base was secured by the multiple patrolling guards and maze-like barrier, all Soldiers carried their assigned weapons at all times. Kyle was assigned an M-16 rifle and carried a magazine of ammo in one of his cargo pocket.

The spotlights assisted in showing him the way back to his tent, but darkness surrounded him in a scary, yet serene kind of way. He felt sort of overwhelmed as he missed aspects of home back in the United States and thought about what would be next. Soon, he would be leaving the somewhat sheltered living of Kuwait and heading into the regional hot spot of Iraq. The intelligence reports that Kyle and his staff section were producing gave estimates and trends made him slightly anxious.

It was late, and he was tired, but he decided that he would sit on his bunk and write a letter to his mom. Though she would never know that she was first to receive one from him, Kyle felt that she needed comforting more than anyone else.

Three days later, those departing to Forward Operating Base Tomahawk were gathered outside one of the tents. Kyle and 72 other Soldiers were listening to the last briefing before the convoy was going to depart. Some seemed eager, perhaps a bit too eager, while some were visibly nervous. Those that were nervous clearly had reason to be. The more recent intelligence trends that Kyle read said that terrorists were trying new tactics against units deploying into and out of Iraq from Kuwait. These tactics included grenades being thrown from bridges, to terrorists taking refuge in some of the mud huts that were sometimes formed not too far from the roads that the units would take. As Kyle listened to the informative, yet jarring, briefing, he oddly remained calm.

Earlier that morning, Kyle opened his eyes with anticipation, but he quickly closed them to say a long prayer for strength for all the Soldiers traveling. He also prayed for the leadership that was guiding them and durability for the vehicles that were taking them to their destination.

The convoy commander for the trip was of the rank Major. He was obviously nervous and speaking quickly in a voice louder than he was used to in an attempt to seem tough and unbothered. He told the Soldiers about to travel about the routes, checkpoints, dismounts and security procedures. Once he was finished, he told all to stand by their vehicle for the final countdown before departure.

Radios were chatting and squelching as last minute communication checks were being conducted. Some of the men were peeing behind their vehicles in preparation for the long trip. Kyle made it to his vehicle and acknowledged everyone inside with a nod. The scene became real to him as he saw two young men kneeling to pray by two vehicles in front of his. Visions from his nightmares flashed through Kyle's mind as he suddenly had to fight the urge to throw up. All of the tactical maneuver and training was about to possibly be tested on that very day. Most of the Soldiers just hoped for safe travels with no incidents, but some others were thirsty at the opportunity to have their first war story. Kyle was more worried about keeping his breakfast down, and he didn't want to look like a vulnerable, scared Lieutenant.

Once the convoy commander swirled his pointer finger signifying that it was time to go, yelps of excitement were heard from some and others were stoned-faced. The time for playing war was over at that point. They were in war…for real. Magazines of ammo were distributed earlier, and everyone about to roll out were loading one in their weapons before entering their vehicles.

One immature Private yelled "Let's go kill some Iraqis! Whew!" He was quickly reprimanded by someone more senior saying, "Get your head in the game, motherfucker. This is not a fucking video game. Someone may die today. It could be you, motherfucker." The smile on the eager Soldier was metaphorically wiped off, and the look in his eyes were a statement of his understanding. Kyle overheard the conversation and almost threw up again. He played it off with a couple of coughs, in case someone saw him, and hopped into the vehicle he was riding in. He kept telling himself, *Kyle, get it together. Kyle, get it together.*

Half an hour later, all departing the base were in their vehicles wearing all of their heavy and uncomfortable military issued gear with their weapons loaded and pointed out of the open windows. As each vehicle was counted off, the front passenger of each made one last radio check and fell in place in the convoy. They had approximately a six-hour ride ahead of them which didn't include breaks or possible enemy engagements. Kyle unconsciously stroked his left leg for a few minutes until he caught himself. Luckily, no one in the vehicle noticed. They were focused outside of the windows, scanning the sectors of their visibility looking for anything suspicious.

Excitement in the vehicle waned as the drive continued and adrenaline levels lowered. Kyle was definitely sleepy, but dozing off was not an option. He read a report that some of the enemies used the tactic of tying a rope on the overpass and a grenade on the other end in order to throw over and swing above upcoming tactical vehicles. He assumed there weren't going to be many bridges and overpasses on the desert highway, but he quickly saw that he was wrong. There were what seemed like way too many bridges, and his muscles tighten as they approached each one.

Even the periodic breaks for accountability and restroom breaks were pretty intense. The drivers were instructed to park on the shoulders of each side of the highway, and upon stopping, each passenger was to hop out, find a position facing away from the highway, and visually scan the area for any distrustful activity. One by one, they would go handle their business either on the road or behind vehicles and return to their positions so the others could relieve themselves. For the guys, it was easy. Kyle noticed that the few women in the unit utilized a small tent without a bottom that was quick to deploy in order to give them privacy they needed.

Overall, the convoy to Iraq was uneventful. Most, including Kyle, were glad to arrive at Forward Operating Base Justice without any excitement and enemy engagement. Truth be told, Kyle prayed the night before that he wouldn't have any personal war stories to tell and wouldn't use any of his combat training unless he had to.

As the last vehicle parked, the convoy commander was heard on the radio calling up his final report announcing the successful arrival of all vehicles, equipment, and personnel. Some cheered and some remained solemn as it concluded. That day, all were lucky, but there none knew what the following days would bring. They unloaded their gear and waited for the next instructions to settle into their new "homes" for about the next 10 months.

Chapter 8

For Kyle's friends back at home, life continued as normal. Rodney was still playing bass in the small band at his church as well as his band. Jasper continued to enjoy single life and make moves at InfoTech Solutions. Mia continued to avoid Greg's advances and flirtations. Once, he tried to get with her under the guise of doing something for Kyle.

Greg texted her one day saying, "Let's put a care packet together for Kyle. I'll stop by to pick up whatever you want to send him." Because it was something for Kyle, she was down, but she handed her monetary contribution to Lamari. Lamari ended up giving the final package to Kyle's father for shipping. She recognized the lame effort that Greg used to attempt seeing her since she would agree to meeting him for dinner or hanging out. She simply was not interested in Greg and would never be.

Though life continued for Kyle's friends and families, the common thread between all of them was their concern for the troops overseas…especially for him. Some of his friends obsessed over the news, while some stopped watching the news altogether. The war had become personal to them and affected them just as much as their hero. At that point in the war on terrorism, too many were losing their lives, and it seemed that the end was nowhere in sight. The updates on the news and in the papers were a daily reminder of that fact.

Within the first month of being at FOB Justice, Kyle had a routine. He usually worked a specific shift while his boss attended all of the meetings – unless circumstances required more of his time at the command center. He worked out at least twice a day, slept when he could, and hung out with Chaplain Mosley. The two men would spend hours talking about life, the important women in their lives, and what they missed about not being home. Kyle enjoyed the talks and mentorship from the older gentleman.

Occasionally, he would meet up with some of his fraternity brothers deployed in the area for lunch or dinner when time allowed for more than two of them to congregate. Some nights involved waiting to access the slow internet at one of the recreation centers or waiting in a long line at the phone trailer twice a week just to call someone.

He rotated calling his parents and his friends with updates and asked them what they were up to on their side of the globe.

Half of his phone calls went to Raven, and she answered most of the time despite the time difference. Kyle enjoyed those late night talks, which were very early for Raven, and felt that their bond was definitely growing from overseas. He questioned his feelings a few times and hoped that he was not being overzealous in his amorous development. He remembered hearing stories from his dad about the "Lonely Soldier Syndrome" and overheard stories amongst some of the younger soldiers as they fell for some random pen pal or got married right before deploying. It was often a topic that came up between him and Chaplain Mosley.

Within the first month of Kyle's arrival, two Soldiers stationed at FOB Justice were killed in the region they were supporting. One of the Soldiers was killed by an improvised explosion device, or an IED, while on patrol outside of the base. He was the same age as Kyle. The other was shot twice in a gun battle while raiding the house of a suspected Al Qaeda leader. The one killed by an IED was in Kyle's unit, and the other was in another unit. Kyle didn't know either personally but went to both memorial services. Chaplain Mosley gave a riveting eulogy for Specialist Thomas "Frog Lip" DeMarco from 53rd Field

Artillery right before the Soldiers were asked to walk by and give a final salute to his boots, rifle, photo, and dog tags.

The next day, Kyle attended the Commander's evening update with his boss just to stay in the information loop. It was a pretty routine meeting other than how the meeting ended. LTC Bloomberg seemed awkward and giddy as he attempted to give a motivational speech to his staff with the main subject of Specialist DeMarco's untimely demise.

"You see sometimes…we…are going to lose folks. That is just a part of war. We…lost one…but…we will probably lose more. We just got to get ready for that," LTC Bloomberg said to a shocked audience as he was beaming s bright, excited smile. In his attempt to "rally the troops", he exacerbated the gloomy feelings that some Soldiers and staff had after having lost one of their own. Kyle was shocked by his demeanor and casualness to death. Kyle had to recover after feeling his jaw drop while he wondered, *Does this guy enjoy this shit?*

The Commander's face was flushed red with enthusiasm as his smile widened as he continued, "We have to go out….and…simply kick butt. It is just that simple. We will….lose…more….guys. Like I said, this is war." The Chaplain coughed loudly, and it was enough to snap the commander from saying anything more. "Ok, folks. Get back to work. HOOAH!!"

They all stood and saluted marking the official end of the meeting. Kyle went to eat dinner at the dining facility with his boss, CPT Cueva. It was rare that they had time to hang out other than their office. CPT Cueva was always intense and usually kept to himself and didn't interact much socially. Kyle assumed that the Commander's speech actually did rouse some feeling from his boss for his subordinate.

Days later, Kyle was doing a leg workout at a gym further away from his command post. The one near his sleeping quarters started to get full at certain times, and he preferred to work out without waiting for equipment or people jumping in on his sets. Most of the equipment in there was in great condition, and there were more air conditioners installed in that gym.

He noticed a woman looking just a bit too good to break a sweat as she rode a stationary bike. He paid particular attention to her because she was paying a lot of attention to him. She had a creamy caramel complexion with seductive eyes and a set of complimentary luscious lips. He figured that she was an enlisted

Soldier for there were not many female officers around, especially cute Black ones.

She continued to stare every so often and finally spoke to him with a simple "Hey," as she exited the gym. He looked at her butt as she walked and scrunched his face up as only Black men could to show appreciation. Whether she was enlisted or not, he could look as long as that was all the he did. Those luscious "soup-cooler" lips of hers would probably talk too much if he were to engage in conversation or anything more than that with her. Fear of getting in trouble and his growing affection for Raven dissolved any further thoughts. He eventually finished his set, grabbed his gear and headed back to work for a few hours.

On the walk back, he saw the girl from the gym in the distance talking to some folks who were also in their physical fitness uniforms. She didn't see him, and Kyle stole a few glances on the sly before turning the corner. He thought to himself how many guys were already trying to stake their claim with her. Kyle's father used to talk to his son about some of the women in the military during a deployment. He called them "Desert Princesses". They were the women, regardless of attractiveness, that all the guys seemed to flock to during a deployment. All the stories ended with jealousy, fights, or someone getting in trouble during or after a deployment.

Chapter 9

Raven was missing Kyle a little more than she thought she would as the months continued. She enjoyed the early morning conversations and napped before the anticipated ones so she could be somewhat coherent during their phone calls. Even from such a great distance, Kyle inspired her to be a better officer. She daydreamed about how life would be if they were to one day become a military couple. She smirked as she envisioned things like both of them coming home each day complaining about their bosses and shining their boots together after dinner.

Raven even took it a bit further by writing a letter to Kyle's parents. In the letter, she introduced herself and gave some background about how she met their son. She then went on to say how much she supports him and how much she was looking forward to meeting them one day. Multiple versions were written and thrown away before she actually mailed it because she wrestled with how her tone may be perceived. She didn't mention the letter to her deployed boyfriend and decided to wait to hear his response when his parents told him.

Her days stationed at Fort Hood were filled with as much excitement, nervousness, and on-the-job training to be expected

of any 2nd Lieutenant. Her unit was not on the timeline for
rotating units due to deploy any time soon, and she was happy
about that. She made a few friends locally and mostly hung out
with them after work.

Raven was the first one in her family to both graduate
from college and serve in the United States military. That
instilled a sense of pride in her and motivated her during the
rough moments. She felt that she could be an example to her
younger cousins and other family members through success in
hard work. She worked hard to be as good as she could be
professionally more to prove something to herself than to
impress others. Kyle was attracted to her drive and
determination for it was indicative of himself.

Kyle also starting writing more letters, too. He wrote
separate letters for his mother and father, but he mailed them in
the same envelope. He mostly wrote Mia because she wrote him
the most letters. She usually gave updates on how things were
going in Georgia as well as updates on his two homeboys there.
She also made a point to drop a flirt or two in each letter, which
always made Kyle smile. Every blue moon, he wrote a letter or

two to Rodney and Jasper, but never expected one back. Jasper usually replied with an email.

There were other folks that he wrote letters to, but the aforementioned were the usual suspects. Kyle, like the other Soldiers, anticipated letters as a way to stay connected to those back in United States. Several elementary schools, churches, and private organizations would send care packages and letters, usually through the Chaplain services. Because they weren't addressed to anyone in particular, they would be disseminated to anyone who was willing to accept them. They were always appreciated as they helped to boost a soldier's morale.

During one of the many conversations that Chaplain Mosley and Kyle had about the women in their lives, Kyle was asked about any other potential women in his life. Kyle told him about Mia and his ex-girlfriend, Brianna. He talked about Mia from the perspective of how she always had his back and constantly tried to open up the door for something more. Brianna was his high school sweetheart that he occasionally hung out with during the holiday visits back home. After explaining his feelings about both girls, he quickly came back to Raven and told him how different she was from them.

Chaplain Mosley suggested that he take a few minutes and write them each a letter to either tell them how he feels or to close those chapters. He felt that the young lieutenant possessed genuine and growing feelings for Raven and that it would be a great idea. Kyle initially said, "Ok", but afterwards, he didn't give it much thought.

He also really didn't give much thought to the woman that he saw at the gym that one day. He figured she was one of the enlisted females in the logistics and supply unit. They were positioned further from his command post, and there were more females there.

Little did he know, she was secretly inquiring about him.

Rodney's wife, Katrina, pushed him to send Kyle a care package, but he didn't make time to gather items and stand in line at the post office. He did, however, buy a Pembrook Alumni t-shirt for his buddy, but it remained in a bag that stayed in the trunk.

It wasn't that he didn't want to make time for his friend, but life stood in the way. After the leader of his band, "Dipped in Soul", quit to pursue a solo singing career, Rodney was unanimously voted to be the new leader. Though he was the newest member of the band, he was definitely the most talented musically and took them to new levels of exposure and musicianship.

Not only did that take up his time, he sometimes played bass guitar at his church which helped with making some of the ends meet with his bills. Money was sometimes tight due to fluctuating hours at his regular job. Thankfully they were gracious enough to allow him to work part time so he could pursue his musical interests. Since he decided to drop out of school so his wife could finish after the birth of their daughter, he was still the only source of income for his household.

He sometimes sat on his front porch in Pembrook with a strong drink after Katrina and Ayana went to bed. Katrina never bothered him because she was thankful to have a man who sacrificed so much for her, stayed faithful, and be the family man that he was. She knew that he needed his time to unwind and to think.

Rodney often thought about finishing up school, better opportunities for his household, and getting over the hill of stress and bills. What mostly consumed his thoughts was his music. He was always writing notes on his mental sheet music, remixing songs that the band played, and thinking of new gimmicks to ensure "Dipped in Soul" would be the best act in Memphis. His head would sometimes swim with creativity.

Nonetheless, he always had faith that there were no such things as accidents, and God had a plan for him that was much bigger than his situation.

Jasper's soul yearned for something more. He had no reason not to feel blessed. He was a rising star at InfoTech Solutions who had skills, personality, with some behind-the-scenes help and advice from his senior supervisor and part-time lover, Shelia Bunton. All was well in his world, but he felt that something was missing. Something bigger was meant to come, but he had no idea what it would be.

For reasons unbeknownst to him, Jasper was still fulfilling his desires for more with multiple women. He never saw himself as a player and was never conceited about his popularity with women. It wasn't always that way for him. He spent so many years being the shy, the nerdy and weird one. As he came into his current self, he realized that he was deemed attractive by multiple women, but he was never doggish to those that he chose to be with.

His personal motto to not be a dog to women that he only wanted physically or temporarily got him into much trouble in his younger years. The misunderstandings and wishful thinking of some women he dealt with sometimes led to their heartbreak and anger. He even had a stalker or two.

One night, he sat on his couch alone contemplating the women that came and went during his years of learning himself. He loved some, but slept with and broke the hearts of so many women. He never meant to break their hearts. Some were crazy – like his ex-girlfriend, Tina. Some were not ready when he was ready for something more with them. Some were simply just for fun on a journey of a young man's conquest to explore his sexuality. One of his former flings, Tara, had recently been calling a lot over the past few months. Though he regarded her as the one that might have gotten away, there were too many other factors that prevented him from giving her another chance – at least not yet.

Chapter 10

The strain of war wears down on different Soldiers in different ways. As Kyle was getting more confident at doing his job and was more into a groove, his nightmares weren't as frequent or as intense. In a way, the nightmares served as motivation and turned him into a workaholic. He constantly read any publications regarding operations and intelligence that was accessible to him. To gain insight, he asked questions of his seniors and his subordinates. He listened intently in staff meetings to hear the planning and updates that occurred. His father's advice about not giving the staff, especially the Caucasian staff officers, any reason to discount his worth to the team constantly replayed in his thoughts and nightmares.

Some of the higher ranking staff members noticed Kyle's eagerness and encouraged it. Surprisingly, the only one that looked unfavorably on it was his boss. CPT Cueva was a laidback officer that looked forward to getting his workday over as soon as it started. He performed well and to the commander's satisfaction, but his lack of drive was noticeable too. His lackluster briefings during the staff meetings and consistent tardiness were becoming a problem. On top of that, the younger and enthusiastic LT Scott was constantly in CPT Cueva's ears asking questions and wondering what more could be done to support the Commander.

Kyle wasn't trying to show up his boss at all. He desired and really needed to stay engaged just to keep the madness away. He was often met with comments from his superior like, "LT, why are you trying so hard?" or "Man, you can do that stuff later."

Kyle thought nothing of it and figured his boss was joking most of the time or being sarcastic. Regardless of what his boss said, he didn't change his routine and eagerness to learn. The fear of making a mistake overshadowed any of the boss's comments or opinions.

Often, senior leadership had the additional stress of not being able to share their pains and strains the same ways that their subordinates could. The military culture gives the perception that showing too much emotion or being under a strain is a sign of weakness. LTC Bloomberg was no different in this aspect. He had a battalion to lead, regardless of the internal tussle to keep in touch with his humanity as he often saw and did things that most men never would. Each major decision that he made could mean success in battle but could also mean the loss of someone's son or daughter. His hard exterior that he put up to everyone was a mask for a man that grew up fighting his own insecurities. Now he was fighting to not let it all fall apart. His wife kept him sane and abreast of what was going on with some of the spouses back at home.

Most Army units formed groups called Family Readiness Groups, or FRGs, that serve as support systems for military families while their Soldiers are deployed or in training. It is usually led by the most senior officer's spouse. LTC Bloomberg's wife was proud of her duties and served unselfishly, but she also had a side of her that was nosey and liked to gossip. She started putting her nose in the business of the spouses and reported back to her husband any news that she felt was juicy or important.

There was a tactical phone in the commander's office that the unit's signal officer installed that could call the United States. On some late nights, LTC Bloomberg would call just to hear his wife's sweet voice before turning in for the night, but she would often inundate him with tales of cheating spouses, bad money decisions made by them, and recaps from the way too many "girl's night out" parties led by her.

Sometimes, he was obligated to intervene and consult with Soldiers once he was made aware of an issue, and at other times, he kept what was told to him to himself. Compared to his previous deployments, that particular one seemed especially filled with trifling spouses and drama back at home. There was one particular time where he felt especially conflicted about a matter with a Specialist Sheldon Sanders. The commander learned during one of his late night talks with his wife that Specialist Sanders' wife had an affair, gotten pregnant, and had an abortion. He prayed about whether he should tell him or not, but his anger about the situation couldn't let him keep it to himself. He just couldn't believe how unfaithful and messy a spouse of a deployed Soldier was when he heard the story.

After one of the staff meetings was over, LTC Bloomberg dismissed everyone other than the primary staff officers. He stood up and sighed before stating, in his known car salesman manner, "Team, what I say in this room right now does not go any further than that. I asked the Sergeant Major to grab Specialist Sanders and make him wait outside the conference room door. I want the Chaplain, Sergeant Major, and Captain Marcel to walk with him to my office and close the door."

The staff was intrigued but confused. Bloomberg then looked at Kyle and said, "LT, I need you to get his weapon once I ask him to relax and put it down. Take it to your office.

Lock the door, and open it when I come get you. Ok?" Kyle assumed that Specialist Sanders must have gotten into some major trouble in order to be instructed to secure his weapon away from him. He guess that there was fear that the young Soldier would react violently.

The Lieutenant Colonel sensed the staff's confusion and decided end the suspense. He frowned in anger and blurted out, "His wife was fucking around and fucked around and got herself pregnant."

Eyes bucked and jaws dropped in astonishment.

"Dumb bitch had an abortion and used his military insurance in the attempt to cover the expenses. Because of that, Sanders will eventually hear about it. I confirmed it and want to let him know before he finds out. I want to monitor his reaction and talk to him." His face started to redden as he kept talking. "Captain Marcel, he will not be fit for duty for a while after this, and I want you to assign a buddy to him for a week to observe him and give him a fucking shoulder to cry on. Then come back to me to let me know if we need to send him home. That dumb bitch . . ."

The Sergeant Major slid in the door to inform everyone that the soon-to-be-heartbroken Soldier was waiting outside and was anxious because he was thinking that he was about to receive some award or recognition for something. The commander winced then straightened up his face as he said, "Team, this is it. Lieutenant Scott, you know what to do." He walked swiftly to his office and a mortified staff began to file out of the room passing the chipper Specialist Sanders without looking at him.

As instructed, Kyle carefully grabbed Specialist Sanders' weapon once the Sergeant Major told him to set it on one of the empty chairs. He walked to another office, in utter disbelief. His young mind couldn't understand what he just heard and had no idea what was about to transpire. He could only imagine what the grinning Soldier's reaction would be while his heart broke and his life would be forever changed. He felt sorry for the young man and was just as angry as LTC Bloomberg was.

Chapter 11

"The number of deaths continue as Operation Iraqi Freedom drones on. The Ambassador to Iraq stated in an interview yesterday on CNN that…"

Mr. Scott was in a barber shop as he was hearing the commentator on the news go on about the number of deaths and the progress in the "War on Terrorism". One of the young guys cutting hair, who was known to say outlandish comments, boldly said to another barber, "Bruh bruh, I couldn't do that shit. The fuck I look like shooting ragheads in the hot sun wearing all that heavy gear? If I was over there, I would be the one trying to take one out for each one of us that died. I know you hear me."

The other barbers, Larry and Ernest, looked at Mr. Scott and felt the verbal explosion coming. Ernest, who was finishing up the retired Colonel's haircut sighed and tried to warn the youngster. "Lil dude, that is why you are here cutting hair and leaving that shit to the trained professionals. Just let it go, man. Let it go."

Hardheaded and oblivious to the change in demeanor of the old Soldier just a few feet away from him, the young man kept going, "Shit is too fucked up over there. We should've not gone over there because all those stupid people who signed up didn't know that they would fight those assholes for nothing. I bet that somebody started this shit to get into office or some shit like that."

As the rant continued, Mr. Scott paid Ernest for another great haircut and headed toward the door. The two older barbers stared at the Colonel and waited for his comeback. As he touched the doorknob, the war veteran and father of a future veteran stopped in his tracks. Without looking at the unknowledgeable and angry gabber, he smoothly said as he faced the door, "You should know your audience before talking about something you don't know about. See, I have seen plenty of guys like you . . . all talk . . . and would probably run at the first sign of peril. Man, I'm talking about peril over there in Iraq and here in these Georgia streets. See, I survived them both, boy." The offender looked around as if nobody was talking to him. Mr. Scott kept talking, holding back what he really wanted to say. "You wouldn't make it over there, so that is why people like my son are over there now and old fellas like me went back in the day. Because of us, you can feel safe telling stories of women you probably didn't fuck and keep lying about doing whatever else you talk about up in here."

After that he walked out and shouted, "Ernest, I will see you in two weeks" as the door shut behind him.

Ernest looked at the youngster and said, "Lil dude, that man must've been in a good mood because... hell . . . I was expecting him to get into your ass for talking crazy like that. Just shut up and cut hair before he comes back in here and slaps your dumb ass." The other patrons exploded in laughter at the embarrassed barber's expense.

Upon returning home, Mr. Scott was greeted by his wife who was nagging him about sending a response to the introductory letter that was sent by Raven. He asked, "Baby, did you already write something?" As she nodded her head he continued, "Well, it's done then. No need for me to say anything."

Not taking no for an answer, his better half stated, "Umm, you do need to say something. This sweet girl took the time to write, so we should too. Give her some career encouragement or something. At least write a quick note to put in my letter." She was unrelenting and knew that he would eventually concede.

"Ok, ok. Damn! Alright, I'll do it, but you can't read it. Ok?" Mr. Scott didn't want to, but he had been thinking about something that he wanted to convey to the object of his son's affection. He asked his wife to grab a sheet a paper from his office.

Once he got the paper, he stared at it for a couple of minutes mentally rewording what he really wanted to say. He thought back to when he first met Raven at Kyle's military graduation. Finally, he started writing while Ms. Scott was lingering around and trying to be nosey.

LT Montgomery,

Thanks for the thoughtful note that you sent us. I hope that you are learning a lot in your initial years in an exciting and challenging career choice. May you walk with pride each day you put on your uniform, and always remember to take care of your Soldiers regardless of your job.

I do want to caution you to one thing. I love my son more than anything, and my every desire for him is that he is as successful as he can be. In saying that, it has become clear that Kyle has become quite smitten by you. There is nothing wrong with that. I hope you are both happy. I will tell you that I was concerned about his decision to have such a new relationship while he was deployed. I thought that he had a case of "Lonely Soldier Syndrome". My years in the Army taught me that is common amongst troops either before or during a deployment. My years in the Army also taught me that the only cure for this condition that he may have is that you either really be there for him or leave him completely alone if you are not completely into him.

Again, thanks for the note. May your career continue to be successful.

> *Respectfully,*
>
> *COL R. Scott, Retired*

He quickly folded it up and placed it behind the letter that his wife wrote. To avoid her temptation to read his note, especially the second paragraph, he sealed the envelope that she already addressed.

Mid-deployment rest and relaxation trips were beginning throughout the unit. The two week period of leave was promised to each soldier and was much anticipated. Most went home to see families while some took leave in foreign lands like Germany and other sponsored resorts in places like Kuwait. Kyle being unmarried without children, placed him lower on the trip's priority list. He was fine with that as long as he knew that he was still going. Per the latest version of the ordered list, he was due to go in a month or two.

He tentatively planned it out, as he did most things in his life, about how he wanted to see Raven first before spending most of his time in Georgia with his parents, Mia, and his boys. Both Jasper and Rodney said that they would try to fly to Georgia if given enough time to prepare.

Daydreaming about what would happen while on leave would keep him motivated in the next few weeks. His boss was scheduled to go on leave in the next few days. That would make him in charge of the staff section during his absence since he was the next highest in rank. Some of the senior enlisted felt that the young lieutenant should have gone before the Captain since he was new to the Army and combat, but Captain Cueva didn't care. He was only thinking about lots of beer, screwing his fiancé, and getting away from his job for a while.

Chaplain Mosley relished the conversations with Kyle just as much as Kyle needed to converse with the older experienced man and officer. From time to time, Chaplain Mosley would ask Kyle to accompany him while spoke with the unit and friends of a deceased fellow Soldier in preparation for their memorials. As time continued for them in Iraq, Chaplain Mosley quickly became the more popular of the chaplains currently at FOB

Justice. His soulful delivery and unpretentious nature made him likeable, and his designated times to preach at the FOB Chapel were usually the most attended. Kyle often attended his services when he could. He took a seat in the back with the Bible that his mom gave him.

One time, Chaplain Mosley was asked to do the memorial service for Staff Sergeant Gloria Hernandez-Ruiz who tragically died while on a resupply mission at a nearby logistics hub close to FOB Justice. She often was a regular attendee to the Chaplain's services and sought him out from time to time to talk. Chaplain Mosley told Kyle that she was a divorced mother whose child was living with her ex-husband and his family. Kyle, the Chaplain, and the Chaplain's assistant went to meet a few of Gloria's battle buddies to gather pictures and select the music that would be played at the memorial service.

Sitting in the trailer, where Staff Sergeant Hernandez-Ruiz once lived, were her former roommate, her immediate supervisor, and Staff Sergeant Melanie Sheffield, who was the gorgeous woman that Kyle saw in the gym that day. As the men walked in the trailer, Kyle lost his breath for a second when he and Melanie made eye contact. They finally knew each other's rank, but their professionalism and the reason for the visit made the eye contact brief.

Kyle noticed that the part of the room where Gloria stayed was segregated by a couple of sheets. Her roommates hung them so she wouldn't see that side of the room; it was too painful. Behind the sheets, everything was untouched and would remain that way until after the memorial. The personal effects of the deceased would be sent home to her next of kin. On the walls were pictures of her son and a poster of her favorite pop star, Justin Timberlake. On the floor, there was a half empty bottle of water and a few full ones. The bed was unmade and her laundry bag sat in a foldable chair in the corner.

After a quick prayer, Chaplain Mosley began his interview of those in the room. He previously had a conversation with her unit's commander and Chaplain. The soldiers closest to the deceased could bring insight to who Staff Sergeant Gloria Hernandez-Ruiz truly was, inside and outside of her uniform. The Chaplain would incorporate the notes into his speech at the memorial service.

Kyle was damn near in tears himself as he listened to the ladies and supervisor talk about memories like how loud Gloria's laugh was or how she would near the line of insubordination when tasked to do something close to end of a workday. Captain Mosley patiently consoled the group and continued down his list of questions. When asked what her favorite song was and what she would want to hear at her memorial, everyone including

Kyle but not the Chaplain broke down in tears as Melanie said, "I think that she would want to hear *Cry Me a River* which was sung by Justin Timberlake."

The roommate looked up at the poster on the other side of the trailer then ran out of the room crying. The Chaplain's assistant, Specialist Wilson, followed to check on her.

Minutes later, Kyle followed the Chaplain back to the vehicle as they got ready to head back to their side of the FOB. The Chaplain's assistant was smoking a cigarette when the two men approached.

The Chaplain jokingly, yet sternly said, "Um…Specialist Wilson, where's your weapon?"

Caught up in what just transpired, Specialist Wilson didn't realize that he didn't have his assigned M-16 rifle on him. "Oh shit. I mean, I'm sorry, sir. I will go back and get it."

Since the Chaplains weren't allowed to carry weapons, their assistants doubled as their protection too.

"You better be glad that I got the L-T here to have my back in case the bad guys come get me," the Chaplain joked as his assistant ran off to retrieve his weapon. In a lower voice, he continued, "I can't fight 'em off with just my good looks. I can't do it by myself."

Just then his voice trailed off, and the Chaplain said again, but with a different meaning, "I can't do it by myself." Kyle looked up to see tears coming down the face of the bald and dark-skinned messenger of God. "Lord, I can't do it by myself. I need you to make a way for the hurt souls, the broken homes, the . . .,"

Kyle was frozen not knowing whether or not he should console the friend that consoled him so many times while he stood praying during his brief bout of helplessness. Instead, Kyle stood there just as pained, feeling just as helpless.

Kyle returned to his room and found out that he received a package from Brenda Scott, his mother. After a rough week and the day's events, he was excited to receive it. Various snacks and magazines were tossed in it along with a letter from her. Also, inside the package was a smaller box that had a teddy bear crammed inside of it. There were a pair of thongs wrapped around it and a note. Mia had sprayed quite a lot of perfume on a red pair of her thongs and the note that said, *"Something to*

help you while you are thinking about me and masturbating,
Soldier Boy – Your sexiest friend, Mia."

Kyle laughed loudly at the boldness of the statement, but appreciated the gift nonetheless. It was good to smell something other than the smell of dust, Port-a-Potty's, and the general dull smell of Iraq overall. He sniffed it a few times before he put it back in the box and in one of his bags. He placed most of the snacks in his locker that was in the room and kept the rest in the box to share with others in the tactical operation center where he worked.

He sat on his bed daydreaming of playing with Mia's big, redbone behind in the thong she sent. Subconsciously, out of guilt, he thought about doing the same with Raven before he suddenly thought about seeing Staff Sergeant Melanie Sheffield in the same thongs. As he got more aroused at the thought, he remembered seeing her crying earlier that day during his trip with the Chaplain. The memory sobered his mood and snapped him out of his daydream. He thought about jacking off but was too mentally tired to proceed. He was so exhausted that he only took off his boots before he laid across the bed and fell asleep shortly thereafter.

He didn't have any nightmares that night, but he did have a dream or two of the young Staff Sergeant in ways that he shouldn't have.

Chapter 12

Months had passed since Kyle and the other Soldiers of 53rd Field Artillery arrived at FOB Victory. Time lost its relevance as the days smeared together, and the weeks really didn't have weekends anymore. The bad guys didn't care if Soldiers wanted to watch a bootleg movie in your room or if they just received some good news from home; everyone was always on alert. Relaxation was just a slight change in the state of mind.

At the same time, people found creative ways to help break up the routine. It was common to see groups of uniforms meet up to enjoy the "surf and turf" day at the dining facility. Card games, like Spades, flag football, and video game tournaments, sponsored by the FOB Morale, Welfare, and Recreation (or MWR) coordinators, kept Soldiers entertained and gave them something to look forward to between missions. Romantic relationships started brewing, whether secretly or openly, between Servicemembers and often were the subject of much gossip.

Lieutenant Scott gained the respect of several soldiers and rightfully so. He was hardworking and smart. What gained him

more popularity was a small tradition he started. His tradition
was to purchase some of the cheaper cigars from the small
shopping exchange of the FOB and smoke one or two on Friday
nights with a group that came to join him. He always brought a
couple of extra for those who didn't have their own or if they
invited others. The premise of the smoke session was to give the
Soldiers time to talk about anything unattributed whether it was
about their leadership, their spouses, the deployment – whatever.
Kyle mostly listened and kept his complaints to a minimum in
case someone had the urge to regurgitate what he said.

The smoke of Swisher Sweets, Black and Mild, and
Backwood cigars wafted in the air along with cigarettes as they
smoked by a very large rock within the FOB. The spot was
perfect to let those talk without fear of repercussion. The line of
disrespect was never crossed, because Kyle wouldn't let it.

Conversations ranged from wives at home spending up all
of the extra deployment money, sport teams, "who is the baddest
chick" debates to who amongst the leadership doesn't know their
job. The conversations mostly made everyone laugh, but there
were tears sometimes and cursing. Regardless, all walked away
feeling a little freer and a little less stressed. For Kyle, he often
walked away with deeper motivation to be better to make sure all
of those guys would return home safely to kiss their wives,
watch the Dallas Cowboys in their own living rooms, watch

Halle Berry in an upcoming movie, or get promoted to another section away from Sergeant First Class Taylor – as one particular person expressed.

Some days, the heat was unbearable in the deserts of Iraq. Despite the fact that six months had passed, no one ever got used to it. Those who worked in the offices aptly, called fobbits, were thankful they weren't in the heat as much as those on dismounted patrols or in congested tanks. Those soldiers wore full battle gear including plates that were meant to stop or cushion against bullets or other small projectiles. Regardless of the heat and heavy gear, the war carried on. The terrorists still placed IEDs and conducted ambushes in that 140 degree weather. That meant the United States and their allied forces couldn't stop just because of the heat.

On the other side of the world, Raven was going through her own war…a mental one. The summer was starting and the heat around Fort Hood brought social activities that kept her busy and surrounded by temptations that she had a hard time resisting. She stayed true to Kyle, but her desire to be touched was just as enveloping as the heat of the sun. Other officers around the base and in the surrounding area took notice of the dark chocolate, flawless-skinned cutie who had the Lieutenant boyfriend overseas. Most male callers respectfully went away once Raven announced her relationship status, but some were persistent and saw an opportunity in Kyle's absence. The letter she received from his father didn't help her struggle as well.

Kyle stayed consistent with sending flowers to Raven each month as a token of his fondness. It was unlike his character to do romantic things like that, but Kyle's dependence on her was more than having a girlfriend. The loved ones at home were the much needed link that he needed back to the world that he knew. Maybe his dad was right about his prognosis of having "Lonely Soldier Syndrome", but Kyle would never admit it. He saw her as more than a link to home and the world outside of the Army, and he was optimistic about a long-term future together.

To some of the Soldiers, war sometimes felt like a never-ending video game that repeated itself over and over again. Even though there were comforts and morale raising amenities in Iraq, they didn't compare to eating greens and cornbread that a mother cooked or the taking a drive down the street in a car to get a Whopper. The boredom of flipping channels on a Friday night from the couch felt echelons better than eating the juiciest steak in Iraq with your weapons inches away as the soundtrack of occasional gunfire played in the distance.

Jasper became more obsessed with watching CNN every day after work. The channel's coverage of war seemed over the top, in his opinion, but it was enough to keep him tuning in day after day. Even though he stayed in contact with Kyle via occasional email or phone call, it became routine to watch for Kyle's name on the ticker scrolling at the bottom of the screen showing the names of those that were reported killed in action. He would watch the names scroll twice with a slight sinking feeling. After the ticker went through the list of names twice and he didn't see Kyle' name, he could then confidently change the channel.

One particular day after watching, Jasper decided to call Kyle's mom for one of their occasional talks, which happened more frequently since the start of the deployment.

"Hey there you! How are things going?" Ms. Scott said when she answered the phone.

"Ma'am, things are great with me. How are you and the Colonel doing?" Jasper thought highly of Kyle's parents and felt that his friend was a weird mixture of both of them. Serious and straight-laced like his father, but overly protective and sensitive like his mother.

While they conversed, Jasper remembered the first time that he met Kyle's father.

Alone in the college home he shared with Rodney and Kyle, Jasper heard a knock on the door. He answered it and saw a tall and more mature version of Kyle who walked right in without introducing himself.

In the same strong, monotone voice as the younger Scott man, he said, "Is my son home?"

"No sir. Umm, do you want to wait on him? He should be out of class already." Jasper wasn't intimidated, but the tough presence of Kyle's father was sort of unsettling and awkward.

"That's fine, young man," was the older Kyle's response as he closed the door. Upon closing it, a picture fell off of the wall shattering the glass of the frame. Without a thought or a word, he pulled sixty dollars from his wallet and handed it to Jasper. Then, without asking, he started walking down the hallway toward the bedrooms. His next words were, "Can you show me his room?"

Snapping out of his flashback, Jasper continued to listen to Ms. Scott. She paused after their typical small talk, and said "He's worried about you." After waiting a second for a reaction or question, she continued, "He keeps saying that you are trying to find yourself or something."

Jasper sighed upon hearing that and said, "Kyle wants me to focus on my career more, and he thinks that I am still all upset over Tina, but I'm ok."

She interrupted, "You probably won't tell me, but what is wrong? Are you really ok?" She knew that part of being 20-something was self-discovery, but her son was worried that Jasper would go astray and limit his potential.

"He has always been all work and little play. Ma'am, I can't put my finger on it, but there is something greater for me than working at InfoTech Solutions. I just don't know what it is." Jasper jumped ahead of what he felt the second point that his friend's mom was going to make. "I'm not going to quit yet, and I don't have too many girlfriends."

She smiled at the second part and said, "Ok, baby. You just be careful with what you doing and who you are doing it with. And don't work too hard." She didn't want to push too much, but she was speaking from the remembrance of her youthful mistakes before she met Kyle's father many years ago.

They continued for a few more minutes before ending their conversation that ranged from the Atlanta Falcons to Kyle's upcoming trip back home for mid-tour leave. Neither of them spoke about the anxiety that came from his friend and her son being in Iraq.

Chapter 13

One Sunday, Kyle was listening to music on his big clunky MP3 player that he bought prior to his deployment. He was usually off on Sundays unless a situation called for his presence in the operations center. He would spend that time usually with a workout after hearing Chaplain Mosley preach at the chapel. The rest of the time was usually spent sleeping and listening to music.

That day he was looking through some of the letters that he received. He sifted through the stack to find a few from Brianna and Mia. He had decided to take the chaplain's advice and write both his ex-girlfriend and his close friend a letter and close those romantic chapters of his life.

Brianna's letter to him was as he expected. It was cold and had a kind of matter-of-fact feel. The response to Kyle's letter spoke of how he wanted something more after high school, but he didn't think that she wanted to continue. He told her that he almost called her to hang out when he was at home, but he didn't want to disrespect his girlfriend.

Part of her reply was:

Well, if you didn't say nothing, then I wasn't gonna say nothing. You weren't worried about me when you went to Pembrook though after high school. You would come home and get this good pussy, but you didn't take me with you though. It's cool though.

Kyle could hear her voice and envision her mannerisms while he read her letter. He thought to himself, *Yeah, that was some good pussy . . . for real.* He smiled as he continued reading.

Yeah, Lamari told me that you came through Atlanta before you left. You didn't even call me. Probably because of your little girlfriend. It's cool. I don't really get down with military men anyway. You know how you guys are.

Kyle completed reading the letter again and thought about that closed possibility. She was cool to party with, but he was determined to be a great officer. He wasn't sure if she could handle the responsibilities and expectations that came with being a military spouse. The letters that he and Brianna wrote made it clear that their past was pretty much over and no future would come from it.

After listening to the R. Kelly remix to Janet Jackson's *Anytime, Any Place* until its completion, he push the button to listen to it again. He became lost in the mood of the music and thought about his days in the Pembrook Marching Band. *Anytime, Any Place* was his favorite song played by the band as a concert piece in the fall of 2001. He was one of the drum majors that year, but as a former trumpet player in the band, he would get jealous whenever he heard the trumpets playing the chorus accompanied by the tubas.

He became even more lost when he remembered the video where the honey-kissed Janet was walking around her apartment in an extensively erogenous relationship with her neighbor across the hall. *Damn, I got to get back to Raven!* Kyle thought to himself as he changed the song on his player to another one of his favorite R&B hits, *Faded Pictures* by Case featuring Joe.

He picked up Mia's letter but was tempted to put it back down. The last time that he read it, he almost questioned why he was with Raven. In her letter, Mia talked about how Greg would never have a chance because she always hoped that something would spark up again between her and Kyle.

She went on to say:

Look, I know that you got something with your current situation, but believe me when I say that I will be around in case she breaks your heart. I may have to break her in the process, but you see what I am saying. I don't know the chick no way.

Kyle always laughed each time at how Mia referred to the various women in Kyle's life. Phrases like, "I don't know the chick no way" or "She ain't got all of this though."

Mia was so forthcoming with her feelings but left herself vulnerable to unfavorable responses and rejection. She didn't care, and Kyle knew it. That letter went on to say:

Why didn't you give me a chance? I thought that I scared you away will all of this thickness or something. I will just be honest with you. I got your back and always will, but you don't want me. It's cool though. I got love for you, Soldier Boy, but you betta not slip. Do you still have that thong I sent?

He knew that his homegirl always had his back and was serious about the "betta not slip" comment emphasizing the point that she would gladly become something more than a friend if allowed. He hoped that it would never be a problem as their friendship continued. As Tevin Campbell's, *Tell Me What You Want Me To Do,* was hitting its climactic point, Kyle scrolled within his playlist until he got to Lalah Hathaway's sweet

rendition of Vesta's, *I'm Coming Back*. He tapped the playback
button to make the track repeat.

He then pulled the latest letter from Raven, but he didn't
read it. He felt that she had been acting differently in some of
their most recent conversations, but he couldn't think of anything
he had done wrong. He wouldn't let his mind go into building
multiple scenarios of possibilities. He had enough to worry
about . . . plus he would be visiting home soon.

The following Saturday, Kyle was scheduled to go home
for his two week leave. Though he wasn't finished packing on
Friday, he figured that he would join the guys.

Specialist Thomas Bond was in a Signal Corps unit that
was stationed on the same FOB, and he had been a regular to the
Friday night cigar-smoking sessions since they happened before
his shift. Specialist Bond saw the lieutenant walking up, and
yelled out, "Damn, sir! You are late as hell."

The Specialist was older than Kyle, but Kyle threw back
at him, "Young man, we don't do all that shouting and shit out
here. I'm only out here for a few minutes. I gotta go finish
packing."

Bond didn't want to seem disrespectful or get in trouble. He understood the officer's hesitance to continue the vent sessions with mostly enlisted Soldiers, so he apologized, "My bad, sir. Jones was just telling us about the car that he wants to get when he gets back."

The assembly of uniformed men carried on as usual with the ritual of laughing, smoking, storytelling, and different discussions. Oddly, Kyle felt sort of guilty for leaving them though he would only be gone for three weeks which consisted of the actual two weeks of uninterrupted leave and about a week of total travel time in and out of Iraq.

Jones talked about the yellow Cobra Mustang that he wanted with the matte black leather interior. Most of the guys jousted him about the high car payments and that he wasn't cool enough to drive a car like that. Playful insults went back and forth, but smiles were seen by the passersby.

Little did they know, one of the hired local men that worked in one of the FOB's laundry facility was watching them. He had been checking them out for the last few Fridays, staying in the dark, giving the appearance that he was smoking cigarettes and talking on his cell phone. No one really took notice of Aqeel Abboud while he gave GPS coordinates and environmental information to someone on the other end of his call. The coordinates he gave were near the large rock where Kyle and the armed Soldiers relaxed and talked.

Aqeel had become one the trusted locals who was allowed to come into the FOB to support the war effort to do various jobs. He smuggled in a small GPS and used it to get readings for a cell of insurgents he had joined a while ago. His older brother had been an insurgent, but was killed at the beginning of the conflict in Iraq. Afterwards, he joined the cell in order to avenge his fallen brother. Per instructions of the cell leaders, he applied to work on the base and worked hard washing the clothes of those who he considered his enemies. He had a clean record of no crime or terrorist activities, so he was able to pass all screening criteria with no problem.

For several nights after he left work, he walked within the area that he was allowed to without an escort, looking for areas in which he could report as possible targets. For several Fridays, he noticed the group of Soldiers congregating around the huge stone, which was several meters away from the living quarters of the hired workers. To avoid suspicion, he stayed far away and gave his best estimate to the position of it based on the readings from the GPS where he stood. He reported to the cell that it would be a great opportunity to "inflict pain for the loss of our fallen".

As Kyle was walking back to his room that night, Aqeel said in hushed Arabic, "Soon, they will feel some of our pain and loss."

Chapter 14

Kyle woke up extra early to get dressed and check his duffle bag for anything that he might need. Before heading out, he packed a few souvenirs that were small enough to fit in his bag without them breaking so he wouldn't have to ship it home later. After he ate breakfast, he went to stand in front of his command post to wait for the bus to pick him and two other Soldiers up in his unit who were going on leave.

At 8 a.m., the bus arrived and drove the passengers to the military airfield where they would wait for hours enduring several briefings and sign out procedures before flying to Kuwait to transfer to a commercial flight. Kyle noticed that several Soldiers were just as anxious and excited about getting out of Iraq for a little while.

Kyle grabbed a couple of the free books donated by various charity groups that had been stacked on a crudely made plywood bookcase. Between sleeping and reading along with a mixture of excitement and nervousness, he figured the flight wouldn't be too bad. After he exited the last line before going to the holding area, he was still shocked that his parents agreed that he should go see Raven first before flying to see them in Georgia. The suggestion worked out perfectly and allowed him time to see everyone that he really cared about in the same trip.

He sat in the holding area, read and ate snacks for hours until the lineup was called for boarding the huge, uncomfortable plane. Almost eight months had passed since he had been back in the states. He was more nervous about boarding the plane to take leave than he was about deploying to Iraq. He had heard from others who already went on leave, that all of the C-17 military planes that were used to fly in and out of Iraq had to take off and land fast to minimize possible adversarial anti-air weapons.

While in the holding area, he noticed that Specialist Sanders walked in looking more like he was redeploying rather than going to take leave. He walked in with another Soldier who was going on leave but was given the extra duty of escorting him home. Sanders was much thinner than the day Kyle was instructed to take his weapon away minutes before he would hear the Commander tell him that his wife had gotten pregnant after cheating on him. Kyle fought the urge to ask, "Are you ok?" Sander's gloomy face had already told him his answer, and it was probably deemed that he was no longer fit for duty and had to return home.

The first leg of the flight was rough; the plane was hot and cramped. Kyle was glad that he packed a couple of tan undershirts, soap, and a travel size stick of deodorant in his small backpack. He was able to wash up a little bit in Kuwait before he loaded the much roomier Boeing 747. Afterwards, he resisted the urge to call Raven out of anticipation, but he waited for he still had a nice amount of flight time before him.

The next flight carried the same passengers plus another group of Soldiers who were waiting in Kuwait. The flight wasn't too long. It landed in Germany where the groups were breaking up to go to several different destinations within the United States and elsewhere. Kyle started reading one of his books, a Stephen King novel, and waited to get his final two tickets. Afterwards, he walked over to a bar where a group of Soldiers were having a beer. Usually, it is not proper to drink while wearing a uniform, but no one, regardless of rank, would say anything to anyone choosing to celebrate their vacation time with a brew or two.

Kyle chose a table away from everyone where a Caucasian man wearing a Dallas Cowboys jersey was sitting.

What would end up being a long, engaging conversation started off with, "Sir, do you mind if I sit here and read?"

The older gentleman looked up and said, "Nope. No problem, buddy."

As Kyle ordered a beer and continued reading his novel, the guy in the cowboy hat introduced himself as Retired Lieutenant General Patrick Walshburn and asked about his travels and how things were going at that point of his deployment. Kyle could tell that he genuinely cared as he was asked, "Are you ok though? War is rough, and you are so young. I was already a Captain the first time that I saw combat."

Kyle looked away as he smiled and replied, "Yes sir. I'm...ok. I'm doing ok."

Kyle was a little star struck talking to the General officer and was visibly nervous. He felt more at ease when he was told to call him Mr. Walshburn. He looked Kyle in the eyes and said, "Stop with all that 'sir' stuff. Right now, we are two men having a conversation and a beer."

Kyle replied with, "Ok, sir...I mean..."

The elder gentleman laughed as he stood up and motioned the waitress to place an order for two more beers. He had the physique of a former Soldier that continued to maintain his level of fitness even though he no longer served. The power that he exuded though was seen in his eyes and heard in his words. It was the same power that Kyle saw in his father and some of his peers. It was the same power that he wanted to be able to project as well one day.

The two officers talked for almost two hours about multiple topics including intelligence operations, the women in their lives, and how to lead Soldiers. They later learned that they were actually on the same flight destined for Chicago. As they announced the flight would be boarding, Mr. Walshburn handed Kyle his business card.

"Mr. Scott, I enjoyed the conversation and the laughs. You are a fine officer, and I'm honored to have met you. Feel free to call me when you need some mentorship." When they shook hands, the retired General squeezed extra tight and said just as firmly, "By giving you that card, it means that I expect to hear from you as soon as your leave is over."

Kyle returned his gaze and squeezed back as he said, "Yes sir." Afterwards, they both boarded and sat on opposite ends of the plane. The fatigue felt from travel was enhanced by the three German beers that he had consumed. Before the front door of the plane closed, he was already in a deep sleep.

Between sleeping and finishing the books he had grabbed, the flight to Chicago was filled with increasing anxiety for Kyle. He thought about how the reunion with Raven would be while he played several scenarios in his head. *Will she be warm and loving, or will she just go through the motions? Will she be free with the booty, or will she hold back?* Those were some of the thoughts that he had during the periods that he was awake. He thought about their matching dark completions melting into each other in passionate and athletic lovemaking to the point that he unconsciously grabbed himself.

He had random thoughts about the homecoming with his parents and his friends, but those experiences were predictable. A lot of food, a lot of drinking, and a lot of talking about the war were on the agenda for sure. He was especially glad that his college buddies were going to meet his hometown friends. He wished that Raven decided to come to Georgia to meet everyone as well, but she was so apprehensive about it to the point that Kyle never brought it up again.

When the plane landed, he damn near ran to the bathroom and just as quickly hopped in the line for McDonald's near his next gate. The Quarter Pounder burger that he ordered was surprisingly not as tasty as he last remembered. He forced the last bites out of pure hunger and not satisfaction as he turned on his cell phone for the first time since he left Iraq. He held his phone for a few minutes to allow it to sync with the nearest antenna. When his phone was synced, various chimes alerted him to the vast amount of incoming voice and text messages.

He read through some of the old text messages and a few new ones asking about his current whereabouts during his travel. He didn't reply to any of them. Instead he decided to fight off his nervousness and call Raven. He wanted to make sure that she would pick him up on time. He also wanted to get a final gauge of her temperament and his emotions. Because Raven took the day off so she would be available for Kyle, it was no surprise when she answered on the first ring.

"Hey baby!"

Kyle felt silly for worrying, and then replied, "I will be there in a few hours."

Chapter 15

Kyle's heart was thumping and his hands were sweaty as he exited the plane at Austin–Bergstrom International Airport in Austin, TX. He was bombarded by several patriotic volunteers cheering, waving flags, and holding signs that had phrases like, "Thanks for Your Service!" and "Welcome Home Heroes!!!" Kyle assumed that someone called forward to the airports to announce that Soldiers were returning home on the flights. People snapped pictures and shook his hand multiple times as he made his way to the baggage claim.

He appreciated the applause and the festivity, but he was focused on one thing... seeing Raven. He read her text stating that she was at the airport. His fingers fumbled as he typed his reply saying that he would see her in the baggage claim area. He was happy to be back in the United States, but he was happier that he would soon see the first woman that he truly ever loved other than his mother.

He shook a few more hands as he waited for the baggage carousel to start so he could grab his duffle bag. Out of the corner of his eye, he saw a figure wearing bright yellow approaching him. He spun around to see his girlfriend holding a small sign and a couple of yellow flowers that matched the yellow ribbon in her hair and the color of her dress. Because she was in the Army as well, she thought that Kyle would find the significance of the yellow ribbon humorous. There was a well-known marching cadence amongst Servicemembers that discusses a woman wearing a yellow ribbon in her hair who waited for her Soldier to return from deployment. Kyle, as well as other former and possibly current Soldiers, picked up on the inside joke and smiled. More applause erupted as Kyle parted the crowd to get to her.

Raven's beaming smile was all that Kyle needed to erase any doubt that he had. At that moment, he truly felt like he was home.

Once in Raven's car, she told Kyle that she had a surprise for him. He leaned in for another passionate kiss before simply saying, "Ok." She bit her lip which sent his level of horniness to another level. He was ecstatic, but was trying to play it cool.

She asked him, "So, are you hungry?"

Considering his disappointing meal, he continued to try to play it cool and said, "Yes. I could eat something."

She saw the desire in his eyes and decided to play with it. "So, do you want some food or do you want to eat me first?"

Speechless, he just stared at her for a second while unconsciously grabbing himself yet again. Raven caught the involuntary action and knew the answer right away. "My surprise is coming up soon, so you decide what you want to eat later. I mean . . . what food you want to eat later." Minutes later, she pulled up to a Holiday Inn hotel. She tried to look coy as she stated, "Umm, I got us a room here. We can go to Killeen tomorrow. If you still feel like going out later, we can go get something on 6th Street."

Kyle's head was swimming in pool of lust, anticipation, and happiness. He lost his cool demeanor for a second as he responded with, "Oooohhh shit! I'm ready for your surprise. You don't know how much I wanted to . . ." He caught himself and then continued, "I don't mind. I am just glad to see you."

After she parked, they quickly got out of the car and headed toward the entrance. Both of the lovers were all smiles and wide eyed as they rode the elevator in silence with an occasional nervous glance as it went up to the 9th floor. Raven sped out of the elevator and headed to room 912. She looked back to see her lover slowly walking behind her. He purposely lagged behind in order to regard the size of her butt and the swing of her shapely hips in the yellow dress that was a beautiful contrast to her dark ebony skin.

She opened the door and walked inside. She was biting her lip again when she stepped out waving at him to speed up. The silent command didn't miss Kyle as he picked up his step and walked into the room. The lamp closest to the door was the only one lit which gave the area of the room where the bed was somewhat of a romantic atmosphere. In the dim light, he saw rose petals scattered across the bed in the shape of a heart.

Kyle had no desire to play it cool anymore, and his body and emotions wouldn't let him anyway. Raven stood near the window and waited for his reaction. He saw two wine glasses on the table, and Hersey's Kisses scattered everywhere. A balloon displaying the words "Welcome Home" was tied to one of lamps. He dropped the bag right after he crossed the threshold of the room and shut the door. His intention was clear when he looked at his lady and said, "Come here."

Raven felt like she was floating as she sauntered to where Kyle was standing. His pants were already unbuckled when she reached the other side of the room. He just about lifted her up when he planted another kiss, filled with love, absolute desire, and longing. He, for quite a while, had a hankering for what was about to happen. All uncertainty and anxiety about Raven's feelings were about to be replaced with sweat and moans. Her dress dropped just as quickly as his pants. Kyle was charged and ready to go as he ushered Raven toward the bed. Once they reached the edge of the bed, she whispered in his ear, "Go take a shower and come back naked."

Chaplain Mosley told Kyle to stop masturbating for at least a week or two before he made it home for leave. "The first one should be kinda quick, young brother. That way she will be happy that you are excited, and it will show that you are not screwing anyone else . . . even if you are." Kyle was glad that he followed the advice though he almost succumbed a couple of times whenever he thought about Raven.

The first one was definitely quick for him. After his shower, Kyle walked out partially wet to a nude and waiting Raven. The air was scented heavily with her perfume. She opened the wine and sipped some as she watched her lover walk toward her fully erect and throbbing. He noticed that she had placed a few unwrapped Hershey's kisses in the valley of her navel. Before he sprang on her, she instructed him to eat the three pieces of chocolate before kissing her.

He gobbled all three kisses at the same time. Once he finished, she had placed the wine glass down and opened her legs. She told him, "I want to taste me and the chocolate." Kyle laughed and caught the hint. He crawled across the bed, for about five minutes he indulged in the essence of Raven mixed with the sugary pleasantness of the candy he just ate.

No longer able to wait, he hopped up and quickly inserted his shaft. Then he popped another piece of chocolate in his mouth and gave Raven what she asked. It turned him on that she wanted to taste herself, and the taste of her wetness complemented by the chocolate turned her on. Despite having a condom on, Kyle climaxed in less time than he had his tongue between her legs.

Raven smiled as he rolled off of her and said in his deep voice, "Get ready for the next round." Still fueled by desire, Kyle didn't need much of a break to initiate sex again. That particular round lasted much longer than the first, and both eventually dozed off satisfied and exhausted.

Shelia was at Jasper's apartment when the phone buzzed announcing Kyle's arrival to the United States via text message. They were just drinking some wine with no intentions of getting physical . . . not that night anyway. The intensity between them was dying slowly, but they still enjoyed each other's company.

She came to drop off a gift that she promised to bring over to him a while ago. She stared at Jasper as he hung up the framed print of a man who was pulling images from his thoughts and formed them out of clay on a table in front of him. Her eyes widened with excitement as the song "Real Love" by Lakeside played from a mixtape that Kyle made from his father's music collection. She was always fascinated by Jasper's knowledge of such smooth, old school rhythm and blues music.

After he hung the print, Jasper went to his phone and smiled when he saw the text message, "It's on now. Kyle's back."

Chapter 16

Kyle was due to arrive in Georgia in a couple of days. Jasper called Rodney and caught him as he was getting ready for a Saturday night set at Jo Jo's Bar and Grill in Memphis. "What's up, J. Hooks? I can't talk long, my brother. I'm getting ready to do, you know, my thing at the spot. You coming through?"

Jasper was preparing himself for the drive to the Scott household coming up and didn't feel like going out. Plus he had another agenda. "Naw man. Ima just chill tonight, but ask Sonya if she can bring you to the crib. If not, call me before the end of your show, and I'll come scoop you up." Rodney smiled as he caught on to what his friend was getting at. Jasper continued, "She did grab you up from Pembrook, or did you drive to Memphis?"

Rodney laughed, "Bruh, I'm all packed, and my bags are in her car. I'm not sure if she really wants to see you, but I'll ask her."

Sonya and Jasper occasionally hung out at each other's cribs even though the excitement between them had faded some over the past months. "Dude, just ask her if she wouldn't mind dropping you off. She ain't got to come in to see me." He said that knowing that she would more than likely come inside even if it was just to talk shit to him. Jasper really was cool either way, but he didn't want to pass up an opportunity to get some of the best pussy that he ever had. Sonya usually didn't pass up an opportunity to play with the energetic young man who would have fully captured her heart if he was older.

Rodney was finishing up his drink as he said, "Ok bruh. I'll ask her and call to let you know between sets. You gonna keep fucking with ol' girl and get sprung. Watch."

Before hanging up, Jasper slyly said, "Naw bruh. Not me. Nope . . . not me. I don't get sprung."

One of the fan favorites at Jo Jo's was Old School Night, especially when Rodney's band was providing the musical entertainment. "Dipped in Soul" performed some fan favorites as well as some new ones that they had been working on. During the middle of the set, Rodney placed his guitar down and walked toward the microphone. He took a deep breath and started singing an acapella version of the 1970s group Enchantment's "Where Do We Go From Here". Rodney's unique rendition sounded nice with the sultry sounds of Sonya and the others joining in. Rodney didn't usually sing, but he heard the song one Sunday as someone was playing it loudly in their car as he was packing up his instrument after church. It was stuck in his head since that day. He had to push it out by singing it acapella. Any other way didn't feel right.

His powerful voice couldn't achieve the higher notes like Enchantment's lead singer, but his falsetto wasn't bad. What won the crowd over was how into the song Rodney was. It was like part of him wouldn't survive if that song didn't escape his lips and the words didn't touch someone's heart in the audience at Jo Jo's that night.

Once it was over, Rodney looked bewildered and still caught up in the moment, and Sonya had to take the microphone to address the standing and clapping crowd. "Alright, Alright! That was our very own Rodney Kirkland taking a break from the bass guitar to pour his manliness and silkiness on the stage and dip you all in unfiltered, grown ass soul. Give him a round of applause!" She looked back at him and saw that he was still looking dazed as he wiped sweat from his face. He was walking back to his usual spot on the stage, and as he whispered to himself, "The music keeps the devil away."

Sonya saw the need to keep talking and made a mental note to ask him what was up with him. "Fellas, I hope you grabbed your ladies hand during that one and sang to her." Various whistles and shouts were mixed in with the applause. She continued, "Ladies, it is now your turn to reciprocate as we keep the Enchantment going on."

She looked at Rodney to see if he had recovered. He had his guitar back on his shoulders and gave Sonya a thumb's up. She caught his eyes and saw into the soul of someone who was way too mature for his age. That previous song's performance was nothing like they had practiced. Older folks who often jokingly believed in reincarnation would probably say something like, "That boy has been here before." She chuckled and thought to herself, *No way could anyone in his twenties feel that song that deeply. What is going on with him?*

Rodney seemed normal as he led the band into a second song by Enchantment. Sonya let out a rousing, "Ohhhh oh ohhhhhh" before she starting singing "Silly Love Song". Most of the crowd recognized it instantly, and some clapped while various sounds of approval were heard as soon as they started.

Kyle and Raven had a wonderful few days together back in her apartment near Fort Hood, Texas. There was a lot of sex, talk about work, cooking, and what-if conversations. Kyle felt totally relaxed and was thoroughly enjoying the much needed vacation. She was allowed to take some time off from work but had to go in for a meeting with her commander a couple of times. Everything seemed blissful, but Raven's eyes were hiding something. Kyle was so in love that he didn't even notice.

She brought up something one night when they were lying in bed watching TV. "Did you tell your dad something about me?"

Not knowing what she was referring to, Kyle answered with frowned eyebrows, "No. Raven, what the hell are you talking about?" She ignored his reply question and continued asking what he could have possibly told his dad until he became irritated.

No longer in the mood, Kyle barked at her and said, "Raven, stop! I don't know what in the hell you are talking about. We talk about you, but I say shit like, 'I like you' or 'we just talked' or something."

Not convinced, she pulled the letters that his parents sent in response to her letter to them. Kyle was visibly angry and confused as she stated, "Baby, I wrote your parents." Kyle's grimace changed from anger to confusion as he wondered why Raven wrote to his parents. She continued, "I thought it would be cool to…you know…umm, introduce myself to them, and this is what they wrote back."

A little leery, Kyle first read the sweet and sincere response from his mother. He smiled and tried to imagine his mother's reaction when she had read Raven's letter. The second page was in his dad's handwriting, but his smile disappeared once he read the end.

Knowing his dad better than anyone, he knew what his intentions were by the words that he wrote. He looked at Raven and said, "Baby, that is just how my dad talks. He didn't mean anything negative."

Unconvinced, Raven sulked a little bit and responded, "But why would he question my feelings like that?"

Kyle recalled several conversations between him and his dad and those that he overheard with his parents about another "G.I. Joe heartbreak". He figured that Raven would have had some to share by now just as he did. Getting a "Dear John" letter while deployed was tragic to a Soldier regardless of their perceived toughness or time in the service. Sadly, it was a common occurrence to those who were deployed with Kyle.

He looked at Raven and pinched her left nipple. Then he confidently said to her, "You don't have to worry about anything. He is just being overprotective. We are good, baby." Inside though, he was seething with rage at the boldness of his father. He made a mental note to inquire about it when he got to Georgia.

The pinching of Raven's nipple turned them both on. Raven suggested that they take a shower before they began fooling around again. Kyle, without a smile and a mischievous look in his eyes, took off his shirt and said, "Grab a couple of condoms and be prepared to get your hair wet."

Chapter 17

Rodney and Jasper argued the majority of the 7 hour drive to Kyle's parent's house. Everything from best rapper to who sang what song first to types of female booties were topics of controversy and disagreement. No true anger, but just debatable topics to past the time. Two things they agreed on were that they were glad to be away from their busy lives for a while to see their college buddy soon.

Jasper timed his departure from Memphis so he would get to Georgia at least an hour before Kyle's plane was to arrive from Texas. They were going to be at his house waiting on him along with Mia and Greg. There would be plenty of food and libations to celebrate their Soldier's temporary return home.

Kyle was explicitly clear in that he preferred not to see anyone else in his circle of friends, family, and associates until he hung out with them first. He didn't want to be bombarded with questions from neighbors and others until he had a few days to relax and let go.

Spearheaded by Greg, the group of Kyle's closest compadres would surprise him by all being together when he walked into his front door. Rodney purposely lied to Kyle saying that they were running late because of Jasper, who was typically late, and would meet up with him later. Lamari would go with the Scott's to pick up Kyle, as planned, while Greg would receive the others. Lamari's car would be the only one in the driveway of the Scott's residence to lower suspicion, and all of the others were parked around the corner of the house. Mia claimed that she would be out of town for a business trip. Greg simply ignored all of Kyle's phone calls and text messages.

As Jasper and Rodney stopped to get their final tank of gas before their arrival, Rodney asked the question, "Do you think that he will be different? I mean, war changes people, bruh. Whatcha think, lil homie?"

Jasper, who was the tallest and slimmest out of the three Men of 1302, hated being called 'lil homie'. He was almost done topping the car off when he looked over to Rodney, who was eating some pork rinds, and said, "Naw, that guy will be ok. We are friends with the future General Scott." The two of them laughed before hopping in Jasper's car to make the final leg of the drive.

Worn out from talking all night and engaging in rounds of friskiness, Raven drove back to Austin to drop Kyle off to catch his flight to Georgia. Kyle thoroughly enjoyed himself and felt a renewed bond with his girlfriend. He really wanted Raven to go with him to Georgia, but he understood her resistance to do so after reading what his dad wrote in response to her letter.

He knew that he would see Raven again, but he felt like he was leaving her behind. He shook it off as he sipped the coffee he bought from a Burger King off of the highway. Between the coffee, the weather, and his excitement to see his parents and friends, Kyle was starting to sweat. The weather was really starting to warm up, and Texas always seemed to have an extra feeling of mugginess.

The agreed plan was that there were to be no tears or extra-long hugs after parking in the short term parking lot at the airport. Kyle ignored it and pulled Raven in to him to spend a few minutes kissing and stirring each other up before departing the vehicle. They walked mostly in silence as they made their way to the check-in counter where Kyle picked up the ticket that his father purchased for him. Afterwards, they prepared to say goodbye before he entered the security checkpoint. Kyle still had a few hours to spare, but Raven had to get back on the road to Killeen.

After one last very passionate kiss, with little regard of the busy crowd around them, a teary-eyed Raven said, "Have fun in Georgia," before she rushed off.   Kyle looked back at his girlfriend a couple of times to see if she would look back. He understood that saying goodbye wasn't easy for her, but he felt slighted because she didn't turn around.

Oh well, Kyle thought to himself as he walked through the security checkpoint. Once on the other side, he bought two magazines. The first was a bodybuilding magazine for new workout plans, and the other was the latest edition of Time magazine to read while he enjoyed a couple of beers at the bar near his departure gate.

In the area of the Hartsfield-Jackson Airport where family and drivers picked up travelers, Kyle saw the beaming grin of his proud dad. His mom fought the urge to cry just as much as Kyle fought the urge to smile. Lamari broke his laid back stance and went up to greet his frat brother first.

"Wassup bruh?!? Glad to see you big timer." Lamari was wearing a reddish-orange bowtie which went nicely with his denim blue colored button down shirt. Kyle smiled at his friend's typically quirky fashion sense that only he could pull off.

Kyle replied, "I see ya looking clean there frat . . . I see ya." Lamari patted Kyle on the shoulder before moving out of his way so he could greet his parents.

Kyle finally broke his stern countenance as he saw his dad still smiling and looking proud. He was just about knocked over by his mom when she approached him. She squeezed him for about a minute before letting go. Kyle grabbed his mom again and squeezed her some more. She kissed his cheek, and said "Welcome home."

As expected, Kyle's father was a little more theatrical and loud as he greeted his son. He walked over with his hand high in the air and slapped it firmly into a handshake as he said, "Look at you boy . . .   looking like a real Soldier and shit! Looking good…looking good." Kyle tried to shake hands with his father just as firmly but wasn't quite as strong.

The two Scott men hugged then shook hands again. Identical smiles, comparative heights, and general size, the two truly looked like an older and younger version of the same person. After a few more words and hugs all around, the four of them walked toward the baggage claim area to retrieve Kyle's duffle bag.

Kyle's mother asked about Raven while his dad asked about the war while they waited. Lamari stepped away to call Mia to let her know to get everyone at the house ready since they would be on the way soon. Afterward, he rejoined them and lied to Kyle about not knowing the whereabouts of his other friends as part of the setup.

"Your mom would kill me and you if you didn't stay at the house tonight. But just in case, I got a room for you for two days to hang out with your boys if . . . you know…you know…," the elder Scott man stated insinuating that wild times were ahead once his son reunited with his friends.

His wife gave him a crazy look and jumped in with, "He just left his girlfriend. He better not be . . . you know . . . you know." Her face softened when she looked back at her son and sweetly said, "Isn't that right, Kyle?"

Unfazed, Mr. Scott rebutted before Kyle could speak, "I don't need the fellas in my way when I am trying to you know . . . you know . . . with you, baby. He doesn't need to see us walking around naked and doing what we do. You know I am right!"

Kyle and Lamari looked at each other with disgust and amusement as his mother blushed. There was a white lady standing behind them listening and sizing up Mr. Scott as he spoke.

"Yuck," came from Kyle's mouth as he grabbed his bag.

Back at the Scott's residence, the two sets of Kyle's closest buddies were getting acquainted while they waited. Rodney felt Mia's eyes on him from time to time while he and Jasper made small talk with Greg. Rodney appreciated the attention, but it make him somewhat uneasy. Subconsciously, he fidgeted with his wedding band and tried not to make too much eye contact with Mia.

Mia noticed the ring, and thought to herself, *Why is it that all of the cute ones are married or don't want me? Damn.*

Mia's bright complexion and thick hips reminded Rodney of his ex-girlfriend, Tasha, who was somewhere in the world striving to become the next R&B sensation. Though she wasn't going to disrespect herself by making a play at Kyle's friend, she had no shame in looking at Rodney's strong arms and the fraternity brands that were slightly visible at the bottom of his short-sleeved shirt. Though he wasn't going to disrespect his marriage, Mia's body was the type of thickness that he liked so he took an occasional glance in admiration.

Greg received the phone call from Lamari saying that Kyle and the family were on the way. He gave the estimated time of arrival. Everybody present in the Scott household policed their items and hid any proof that they were there. They hung out for about twenty minutes more before they went to Kyle's bedroom to hide out.

Rodney's first glance around Kyle's bedroom gave more insight to who he really was. Several awards for athletics, music, and orator competitions hung on the walls and were stacked on his desk. Barely knowing Kyle's father, he wondered how much of his former roommate's past activities were due to his personal interest or were guided by his father's direction and influence. The accolades highlighted Kyle's determination to be the best at whatever he did. Flashbacks about how Kyle executed various things in school now made more sense to Rodney. Whether it was schoolwork, a band performance, or leadership opportunities in his Army ROTC program, Kyle strived the do his best with no excuses for failure.

Mia sat on one of the corners of Kyle's bed still enthralled by Rodney's powerful presence. She thought Jasper was attractive as well, but Rodney's over-the-top nature made him stand out as he interacted with the other two guys. His seemingly powerful hands and his sculptured arms played a starring role in a small daydream that she was having while sitting there. Greg noticed Mia's sudden fixation and sighed in slight jealousy before asking Jasper some questions about his job.

Twenty minutes later, the front door of the Scott's residence opened. Mr. Scott told his son to put his bags up and come down to join them for a drink before dinner. Kyle was texting Raven when he opened his bedroom and was grabbed by Rodney. "Whaddup homeboy!" After seeing Kyle jump into a defensive stance, he realized that grabbing a Soldier with heightened awareness probably wasn't the best idea. It took a few seconds for him to calm down and to notice his other friends standing around with their jaws dropped.

Mia broke the silence with, "Surprise?"

Jasper and Greg followed suit, "Surprise!!" Lamari walked up behind them and starting laughing. Kyle started laughing as well, and they all took turns hugging and greeting him. After a few moments, Kyle's mom called everyone down to grab something to eat.

Ms. Scott had warmed up the lasagna that she made the day prior. Mr. Scott passed out beers and made drinks from his extensive bar. As people made their plates, Kyle silenced everyone and offered to say a few words before blessing the food.

"I am glad that you all were able to make it. Unfortunately, I have to go back to war, but I am blessed to be here with all of you. God saw to it that I had the most important people in my life around me." He paused as he thought about Raven before continuing. "I will enjoy these moments that I have with you all while I am here and go back refreshed. Please bow your heads and let us pray."

After everyone said "Amen", Jasper joked about the eloquence of Kyle's words.

"Ol' Toastmasters speech-giving, junior reverend talking…," the whole crew laughed while Jasper continued making fun of Kyle as he lowered his voice to mimic his diction and mannerisms. "So I want to thank you, thank you, thank you for the cordial, lateral, symphonious, and apparently or seemingly cooperative affection upon the suspiciously accurate gentility…," bringing his voice back to normal, Jasper said, "We love you, mane. Glad to hang out with you again."

Kyle had already downed half a beer and replied, "I don't sound like that." Instantly, all of his friends loudly cackled and disagreed. Rodney boomed in with, "Shhhhhhiiitt! Naw, homie, Jasper got you on that one."

Kyle looked and everyone and continued, "You wouldn't like it if I made fun of all of you." Then he tried to imitate Lamari, but sounded nothing like him and as if he was trying too hard. All were silent for a second trying to take in what had just happened, but laughter quickly erupted again. Mia boo'ed then hugged Kyle as a way of saying, *Nice attempt.*

Kyle was about to imitate Rodney, but Jasper jumped in again with another imitation of Kyle and said, "Ok guys. Come on now. I didn't come back from Iraq to be made fun of." The mention of Iraq kind of sobered everyone in the room into silence for a few seconds. To break the silence, Lamari proposed a toast to Kyle.

After the toast, everyone ate, drank, and talked about everything but war. They all got the gist that the deployment was not on the menu of topics that Kyle wanted to talk about at that moment.

Chapter 18

At Forward Operating Base Justice, Sergeant Bays rallied up the some of the usual crew to smoke cigars at their usual spot. Even though LT Scott wasn't there, Bays took charge in organizing the Friday night talk. Five guys showed up including, Specialist Jonathon Filner, who was Sergeant Bays' roommate. Filner walked up with small box of cigars to share with the crew. His brother, Andrew, a lawyer in Idaho, sent some cigars after hearing so many stories about the "talks at the big rock".

Filner would go on and on to Andrew about things that they talked about and how Kyle made sure no one got too far out of control. Not as extroverted as his older brother, Filner really opened up given the type of atmosphere that Kyle fostered. Andrew was happy to hear that occasional spark in his younger brother's voice because he worried a lot about his social development. He sent two special, higher-quality cigars – one for his younger brother and one for Kyle. Filner excitedly brought them with him Friday, but forgot that his officer buddy, LT Scott, wasn't there.

"Ima wait unit the L-T gets back before I smoke my big one, but you guys can grab one of the other ones. We can smoke those." The other four in the group did just that and lit them. Filner was glad to be accepted by his impromptu group of friends brought together by Kyle. Bays helped Filner come out of his shell and gave him career advice often. That night was no different; smoking, laughter, complaining, and good times.

About twelve minutes after the small assembly of Soldiers starting hanging out, a couple of artillery rounds were heard being fired from one of the buildings about a mile outside of the FOB. The typical notification alarms didn't sound to signify that incoming fire was detected on the base. Once Sergeant Bays heard the incoming projective, it was just about too late. "Damn! Incoming!!! Incoming!! Get to the bunker!"

Though the bunker was fifty yards away, all of the guys ran as fast as they could trying to get to cover. Filner realized that he forgot the box of cigars, and he turned around to get them from the big rock. He grabbed them and headed back toward the bunker when the first artillery round struck the location about 2 yards from where he was. The force of impact tripped up Filner, and when he fell, he dropped the box. When he attempted to stand, the second round exploded much closer to him. The others watched helplessly as Filner was struck by shrapnel and rocks. A cloud of dust rose when he fell back to the ground.

Once the dust settled, Specialist James Zuck was the first person in the bunker to see that Filner wasn't moving. He tapped Sergeant Bays who was already tearing up after having realized the same thing. All were in shock and disbelief; the five cigar-smoking Soldiers just looked at Filner laying still, face down.

Bays finally called out, "Hey Jonathon! Jonathon . . . get up!! Get up damn it!"

Zuck slowly started walking toward the big rock and Filner and noticed others running toward him. Bays didn't move as tears blocked his vision. The other two in the bunker just stood there next to him, unable to move or speak.

By the time Zuck made it to where Filner was lying, the others had run over attempting to resuscitate him. A big knot was protruding from the left side of Filner's head. One of the guys said that he was alive but unconscious. Small cuts were visible on the side of his face. Someone had informed the military police and FOB medical personnel about what happened when they arrived to the location. They escorted Zuck and the others away from the scene to ask questions and to give Filner preliminary medical attention. Bays broke away and walked back to grab the box of cigars that his roommate dropped. All of its contents were still intact.

A day later, Specialist Jonathon Filner was pronounced dead after complications stemming mainly from the head injury that he received. Bays was actually sitting next to his buddy in a military medical facility awaiting for an evacuation to Germany for further medical treatment when he had succumbed to his injuries. He screamed out, "Come on, man! NOOOO!!" as Filner's last breath escaped.

Hours later the same day, two Soldiers pulled up to a house in rural Colorado. A chaplain accompanied Sergeant Major Luccio for what was an honorable, but perhaps the worst duty, to have in the Army; he had to be the one to notify Filner's next of kin. He cried a few tears for a Soldier that he had never met as he got dressed that morning and a few during the hour long drive. He took a deep breath to hold back a few more once the chaplain said to him, "Are you ready?"

Sergeant Major Luccio opened the car door and cleared his throat to prepare himself for the words that he was about to speak. Inside the house, Specialist Filner's father saw the two men exiting the vehicle and instantly knew what was about to happen. He had watched TVs and movies that had the same scenario that was walking toward him in real life. He steadied himself as he opened the door before the Sergeant Major knocked.

Sergeant Major Luccio saw the tears streaming down the face of a father of a fallen Soldier, and choked up as he said, "Sir, I am Sergeant Major Luccio, and I regret to inform you…." No longer able to finish, the chaplain jumped in. Without saying a word, Specialist Filner's dad opened the door to let them in. His wife overheard the men talking and sobbed silently at the dining room table.

Andrew Filner had just finished up with a client when the news came via phone call by his mother. After hanging up the phone, he was still in shock as he walked to his office door to close it for some privacy. He felt nauseous and overwhelmed with what he had just heard. He had just spoke to his brother days earlier when Jonathon called to say thanks for the cigars. The memory of that conversation struck him hard as he felt guilty for not trying harder to push his younger brother to pursue another career choice other than the military. He was audibly crying as he walked over to his desk and slumped in his chair as he angrily said, "I wish he never joined the damn Army. I should have made him listen to me."

"You guys be careful out there, and don't do anything stupid in that hotel room," Mr. Scott said to the group of young college graduates as they prepared to make their exodus.

Rodney answered back for the group, "Sir, we good."

Being the only female, Mia felt compelled to dispel any thoughts that Kyle's parents may have had about her drinking with a bunch of guys in a hotel. She answered back to Mr. Scott, "I don't know what they are gonna do when I leave. I gotta work in the morning."

Minutes later, the group seemed to be milling around and in no rush to leave so Kyle's mother jokingly said to her son, "Dear, your father paid some good money for that suite. If you don't want to go, we will spend a couple of nights there." She had started cleaning up the kitchen and putting the leftover food away.

Without a grin, his father followed up with, "Either way, I'm getting me some. Either here or there, I'm about to grab on your mom's booty after a couple of more drinks."

In response, Jasper's jaw dropped, Lamari laughed, and an embarrassed Kyle said, "Yuck. Ok y'all. Let's go."

Purposely to add more embarrassment, Kyle's dad kept it going, "Yeah son. After we clean up, your mom and I are about to get naked." Then he looked at his wife with pure love, and said, "Ain't that right?"

Mia finished the drink that she was holding and said, "I know that's right! Go head, Mr. Scott! Get it, get it!!"

Kyle who is beyond embarrassed, repeats again with a little more emphasis, "Ok y'all. Let's go!"

As everyone started moving toward the front door, Kyle called his dad over to the kitchen. "Thanks dad for hooking up the room for me. It was cool that everyone was able to make it to see me."

His father nodded and told Kyle, "Son, grab some chips and stuff from the cupboard. Get one of the sealed bottles from the bottom of the bar. Don't take my good shit now. You guys be careful out there.   Do you need any prophylactics?"

Kyle shook his head. He was somewhat offended that his dad brought up condoms knowing that he had a girlfriend that he was faithful to. Maybe his comment was harmless, but Kyle suddenly remembered the conversation that he and Raven had a couple of days ago along with his Dad's letter. Not really wanting to bring it up with his friends waiting outside, he just said, "I'm good."

"Ok, son. We will talk when you get back. Call me in the morning."

Kyle headed toward the door and then looked back to say, "Yep, dad. We will talk."

Mr. Scott watched his son leave and was taken aback by how Kyle said, 'We will talk', but he dismissed it.

Rodney had never been to Atlanta and was fascinated by the view of the skyline and city's lights from the passenger's side of Mr. Scott's Lincoln Towncar. To him, it was similar to Memphis but different in other ways. Mr. Scott had let his son borrow the Towncar even though Kyle really wanted to borrow the Jaguar. Rodney, who was alone with Kyle, took the opportunity to see how his friend was doing and how he really felt.

To ease into the topics that he wanted to talk about, Rodney started with something to get a smile out of his homeboy. "Bruh, it's cool to see that your dad is still getting it on. I betcha he bent her over as soon as . . . "

Kyle swiftly cut him off with, "Whoa! Hold the hell up!" before bursting into laughter. He continued, "That dude is always talking like that and embarrassing me and shit. He doesn't give a fuck who's around. My mom ain't complaining though. Yuck."

After they finished laughing and joking about his dad, there was an awkward silence. Rodney resumed his checklist of questions, "Speaking of bending over …you should be tired from your time with umm . . . what's her name?"

Kyle dryly said, "Raven."

Rodney continued, "Ok. So y'all good, muthafucka? Nothing else to say?" Mocking Kyle's way of speaking, Rodney answered for Kyle and said, "Yes, Rodney, her name is Raven, and she is an exceptional young lady." Converting back to his country twang, "Tell me something playa. All I know is her name, bruh. Damn."

Kyle was riding on Peachtree Street, just minutes away from the hotel. He looked back in his rearview to see if Mia,

Greg, and Lamari's cars were still close behind before regarding Rodney's aggressive inquisition. "Yes, we are good. I thoroughly enjoyed my time with her."

Rodney continued his questions as he sought more erotic details. "So did you guys fuck or just enjoy each other? You know what I am asking? Why you being all quiet about it? She must really be special. Is that what it is, bruh? Huh?"

Kyle knew that he was playing with Rodney who was staring at him waiting on more detailed answers. "Rodney, to answer your questions…both. I enjoyed fucking her." They both laughed and pounded fists. "Real talk, we had a good time. I wish that she could have made it over to meet you guys. You would like her, pimp."

Rodney laughed again, "That's what I'm talking about. My nigga Kyle in this bitch getting some back-from-deployment head and shit." After a few seconds, he looked out the window again and asked, "So are you ok? I mean how are you doing over there?"

Kyle took a deep breath and answered, "I'm good, dawg. One day at a time. One day at a time. I'm ready for it to be over with, honestly."

They parked at the hotel. Even though he had more questions about Iraq, the deployment and his friend's mental state, he didn't want to push. Satisfied with the answers he got from Kyle, Rodney ended his questioning with "Ok."

After checking in, the party that started at the Scott's household recommenced. The Crown Royal bottle taken from Kyle's house was emptying quickly as the guys were mixing it with various chasers they bought. Mia had stopped drinking earlier and was talking to Lamari about various topics. She would take an occasional glance at Rodney who never returned her gaze unless he was speaking to her. Lamari and Jasper had instantly connected earlier as if they were kindred spirits. They mostly hung around each other drinking and telling stories about their dating lives amongst other topics. Their actions, reactions, and even the stories they exchanged that night were similar. Kyle never noticed how parallel they were until that night. Greg mostly kept to himself stewing in his unrequited desire for Mia. Kyle noticed and made a mental note to say something to Greg when the boys were by themselves.

Kyle, partly due to Rodney's pressuring ways, called Raven and put the call on speakerphone. Everybody spoke and made jokes. Even Mia said hello, but thought to herself, *I still don't like the bitch.* The call made Raven feel welcomed, and it was cool to hear the voices of those that Kyle spoke so highly of.

Afterwards, he went into the hallway to speak to her privately. The jeers followed as soon at the hotel door closed.

Kyle's words were somewhat slurry as the liquor brought out his flirtatious side to his girlfriend. "Hey girl! You …you … should be here. Jasper and Rodney are arguing about … about … nothing … again. Greg over here mad because Mia doesn't want him and shit. You would have so, so . . . so much fun." Raven smiled and listened. She liked it when Kyle had a few drinks because he wasn't as serious and tended to be more open. She was happy that Kyle was able to come home and that she was able to spend some time with him first. She had a lot going through her mind, but it was the wrong time to talk about.

After a few more minutes, she ended the conversation. "Baby. Go ahead and join your friends. Call me tomorrow."

He hung up and had a thought. *I think I am in love.* Just as quick as he thought it, he figured that the liquor was coercing his thoughts. *I need to stop sipping. Shit.* He walked back in the room and joined his crew. Mia was saying her goodbyes. "Umm, Soldier Boy, while you were in there getting your Betty Crocker on … caking your woman, I almost left. Some of us got to go to work tomorrow."

Greg remembered that he had to do the same and saw an opportunity to say something to Mia privately. "Yeah big dawg. I need to get out of here too. Mia, I will walk you to your car."

Without hesitation, she hollered back, "Naw. I'm good. 'Preciate ya though." After that, she left. Jasper winced after witnessing the rejection. Rodney was oblivious and sitting in the other room texting Katrina.

Greg tried to play it off and said under his breath, "Man, fuck her."

Kyle dapped Greg and told him, "You know that she won't talk to you because I used to be with her. Nothing against you, dawg, but Mia doesn't want to be *that* girl. You feel me?"

Greg internally felt jealous because that wasn't the only time that his frat brother said something to that effect. He didn't show it and played it off. "Aight then. I will see you tomorrow."

Before Greg could leave, Rodney walked out of the bedroom that he was in and loudly said to Greg, "You out, pimp? You gonna kick it tomorrow though?" Greg nodded. Rodney sustained his loud and tipsy tone, "Ok. Cool. Where da fuck did umm …what's her name? Mia! Where did Mia go?"

Lamari called out from the couch in the common area of the suite, "Big Swole, she had to leave. She gotta work in the morning."

Bluntly, Rodney said to Greg and Lamari, "I know one of you gotta be hitting that. That redbone there! Bruh, one of y'all need to get that. For real!"

Greg replied, "Maybe one day, big dawg. She be tripping and shit." Kyle didn't say anything.

Chapter 19

Lamari, Kyle, Rodney, and Jasper woke up the next day with varying degrees of being hung over. Kyle had no alcohol while he was deployed and had the worst hangover. Jasper kept telling him to slow down, but he felt that he could hang with them. After rolling out of bed, Kyle wished he would have listened. After a couple of visits to the bathroom, he knew he should have listened.

Lamari took up a collection to get some breakfast from the nearest Waffle House and some Gatorade. He was definitely the most able amongst them. When he returned, Jasper was up drinking water and doing pushups and sit-ups. The other two had fallen back to sleep.

By noon, everyone ate and felt better. After showers and getting dressed, the four guys went to Lenox Square Mall to look around and scope out women to possibly party with later. Though Rodney and Kyle weren't really scoping, they played wingmen to Jasper and Lamari who were again hanging tight. After getting a few numbers and some lukewarm promises from some women who said they were coming over later, they left to catch a movie and eat again.

Greg eventually caught up with the guys later that day. The entire time, Kyle and all of his homeboys enjoyed themselves. They revisited stories of their college days and girl exploits, complained about their jobs, and joked on Kyle with imitations and Army topics and imitations were shared amongst them as the day continued. As the sun was going down on the Atlanta skyline, the group re-upped on liquor and food to take back to the hotel suite.

Later, one of the girls Lamari met brought a couple of friends to hang out with the fellas. They were both stunning and brought interesting conversations as well as contributions to the assortment of liquor. Rodney felt like debating and ensued in some controversial topics with everyone jumping in to give their opinion. Kyle liked to play 'Devil's advocate' and did so quite often just to try to stump his friend.

As promised, Mia came later and was glad that she wasn't the only female. She felt bad about not letting Greg walk her to the car. She assumed correctly that Greg was embarrassed by her actions so she made an effort to talk to him more throughout the night. She made sure to check him when his confidence seemed to get too high and he would be suggestive. He would get suggestive with some of his responses to Mia, and he even attempted to rub her left thigh a time or two.

It seemed like each attempt Greg made to show stronger interest in Mia was shot down politely yet firmly. After a while, Greg found solace in talking to one of the women that Lamari invited over. Instantly, Mia felt some type of way about it since she wasn't the center of his attention. She spent most of the night continuing to debate Rodney about music and other things. Rodney felt more comfortable around her obviously staring calmed down since it was understood that he was happily married.

Jasper wasted no time flirting with the tallest of the three new girls that came over. Effortlessly, he kept her laughing and blushing, and he even disappeared in one of the bedrooms with her for several minutes. They didn't have sex, but they partook in some heavy touching and kissing. She was willing, but Jasper convinced her to give him some head instead so they can get back to the party without looking too disheveled or guilty. The girl that Lamari brought over was in the same mood and suggested hanging out with him later in the week when so many people weren't around. As Jasper walked out after his private party, the two players silently regarded each other with a head nod which spoke volumes and like-mindedness between them.

Kyle, like the night prior, was fairly quiet. He jumped in and out of the multiple conversations, but his good time was found in seeing everyone else having one. He thought about work and wondered what his unit and Chaplain Mosley were up to. It was hard to not think about it since his nightmares returned the night prior despite the heavy drinking.

That night, Kyle walked Mia to her car as the festivities continued. When they got there, she used her large frame to her advantage to corner Kyle between the car and the nearby wall. Her eyes were full of wanting as she boldly, yet shyly, moved in close to Kyle's face hoping for a kiss. Reacting too quickly for Mia's comfort, Kyle swung away hard and said, "Whoa! What's up? What are you doing?"

Mia expecting exactly what had just happened said, "Nothing" before moving to get in her car. She stopped before stepping in and looked at Kyle with genuine hurt. She sighed and said, "Look, I am not trying to make things weird and shit, but I wish that you really would have just given me a chance...a real chance."

Kyle's mouth opened up to say something and remained frozen as he was quickly trying to replace the thoughts that he really wanted to say with something less hurtful. His usual blunt nature would have definitely been inappropriate, so he said,

"Girl, you know that you don't want me like that. Besides, ain't I too short for you anyway?"

Mia caught the hint, but retorted in her usual fashion, "Shhhitt. You never needed a ladder to hit this from the back!" She smiled to hide the true hurt that she was feeling as well as the fact that she saw Kyle unconsciously grab himself after her comment.

Kyle replied with, "True. Ok Mia. I'll holla at you later. Text me when you get home." After that, he turned around and walked back toward the hotel without looking back or giving Mia another chance to say something flirtatious.

After checking out of the hotel, the plan was for Jasper and Rodney to stay in Georgia a couple of more days before heading back to Memphis and Pembrook, respectively. Kyle would spend the rest of his two week leave with his parents as planned. The three former roommates and friends for life really didn't do much else but sleep late, sip, eat, and other things to pass the time.

They did spend a lot of time talking and catching up while sitting in Kyle's room. Kyle opened up more about his feelings for Raven, which shocked both Rodney and Jasper. They knew that their homie cared for her a lot, but it amazed them to see their discreet and inexpressive friend be so forthcoming, especially about a woman. Kyle went on and on about their conversations and letters, and he asked for opinions about whether he should see her as "the one". His friends listened and offered their support. It was more so Rodney than Jasper.

"There ain't nothing wrong with love, man. Though Katrina gets on my nerves, I wouldn't have it no other way, man." Rodney was always an advocate for his friends finding the same peace he found with only one woman. Though he sometimes lived vicariously through them as he listened to their wild adventures over the years, he never felt the urge to stray. Seeing his father stray on his mother multiple times, instilled a sense of only desiring one woman at a time.

The talk of love and relationships eventually led to the subject of Tina and if Jasper was getting over her. "Y'all, Tina is still in jail for a lil while longer, and I'm doing me. I have no complaints." Jasper stated nonchalantly even though his face said differently. Kyle pressured him trying to get him to honestly open up. After being double-teamed by the others, Jasper finally stated, "Getting all of this pussy gets boring, mane. I mean, they all say that they only want sex, but then they pull out that hidden contract that they kept in their back pockets as soon as your make them scream or moan. Ya feel me? Then they want to spend all their time all up under me and shit. Crying when you don't call. Crying when you got to go. Crying when you get tired."

Rodney was waiting for Jasper's rant to be over before he said something, but Jasper kept going. "Mane, then . . . then once you start showing them some attention, some of them wanna act funny. You know what I'm saying? Whatever you do ain't enough. Whatever you do isn't right. So and so does it like that. Why don't you do that?" He finally took a breath, and finished with "I'm at the point, mane, that getting some draws ain't even worth it like it used to be."

Rodney paused to make sure that Jasper was finished and candidly told him, "Maybe you should get out the game and focus on one person." After getting no reaction, he continued. "How you really holding up after the bullshit Tina put you through? I mean something is different about ya, pimp, and I don't know pimp. I don't know." Jasper replied again with, "I'm doing me." Then he looked down and out of nowhere said, "The one thing that I miss about Tina is that passion, bruh. I haven't found that yet. I'm talking about that slow jam music playing, toes curling, candlelight, knock-your-ass-out-for-the-night type of passion."

"Alrighty then…ok." Rodney was trying not to laugh, but Kyle understood what his love-seeking friend was talking about. Kyle thought about Raven and thought to himself, *We kinda have that type of passion. I think.* Rodney took a sip from his drink and braced himself for another long-winded answer from Jasper as he asked, "Do you ever think about Tara? I mean, she probably wouldn't mind another shot."

Jasper broke up with Tara to get back with Tina during his senior year at Pembrook. When Tara was a sophomore, she fought to be the object of his affection and passion. Thinking of his future, Jasper chose erroneously and later regretted it. Just when he reconsidered correcting his wrong with Tara after the Tina incident, he learned that she was sleeping with one of his fraternity brothers who Jasper was close with. The blow was too much for him at the time considering that Tina did the same thing with another one of his frat brothers.

Jasper had thought about what Rodney had just said, but he wasn't going to admit that he thought about Tara just then. He looked at his buddies and gave the short answer, "I don't know, mane."

Later that evening, Kyle's father cooked some ribs and chicken on his large grill in the backyard while his mother cooked some of her son's favorite sides. The men drank beers outside and had debates on who had the best barbeque, Memphis or Georgia. Rodney and Kyle's father went back and forth talking about seasoning, sauces, and grilling techniques. When all was complete, the 'Men of 1302' sat down with Kyle's parents. The man of the household blessed the food and everyone started chowing down in silence.

Mr. Scott was already quite familiar with Jasper and took the opportunity to get to know Rodney better. Kyle updated his father regularly about his friends in their conversations so he already had some background. "So Rodney . . . how's the wife doing? Your little girl?"

Rodney waited until he chewed and swallowed his food before talking. "She's good, sir. My wife should be finished with school this summer. My lil girl . . . that's my world, sir. She's good, too. Just growing and eating."

As soon as Rodney mentioned his wife finishing school, Kyle already knew what his dad was going to ask next. "That's great. I hope to meet them one day. What about you? I hear that your band is doing pretty good. So what are your plans for school?" Kyle shifted in his chair not knowing how respectful Rodney was going to continue to be if his dad kept being inquisitive.

Rodney, not intimidated by the tough retired Colonel's light interrogation, chewed up another mouth of food, took a sip of water, and then addressed Kyle's father. "Yes, the band is doing great. We bring Jo Jo's so much business that we were able to renegotiate our contract with them for more money. "'Dipped in Soul' is doing our thing." He paused took another sip then looked Mr. Scott in the eye. "I'm not sure if Kyle told you, sir, but I promised my wife that she could finish school first while I take care of things. Though we weren't trying to, we brought a beautiful lil girl into the world. That changed everything. I had to hustle, but we are never hungry. And I get to keep that promise. She is almost done, and then it will be my turn. Maybe not right away, but one day."

Forceful by nature, the interrogation of Rodney continued. "So, son, are you saving up for it? What does one day mean?" Both Kyle and his mother gave the patriarch subtle, but stern looks. Jasper looked up at Rodney for his reaction. Out of respect for Kyle, Rodney calmly spat back to what was just asked. Normally, he would have been a little more aggressive, but he metaphorically bit his tongue.

"One day means I don't know, but it will happen. First, I got to make sure we can eat and live, aight, while Katrina does her thing. I got three jobs and barely get any sleep, but my women are good. The big one and the small one. Lil sexy and lil mama. As a man, I do what I have to do. No disrespect, sir, but I got this."

Kyle was perturbed and couldn't think of something to change the subject. There was no need though, Mr. Scott was grinning widely. "Ok young man. I respect that. I really do. I wish you luck, son. I feel that you can do it. I had plenty of Soldiers and leaders in my day, and not too many would look me in the eye like you did."

Rodney thought to himself, *I don't need your respect muthafucka.*

Jasper was the first to see Rodney's expression change. He thought to himself, *Oh shit! Shut the fuck up, Mr. Scott.* Rodney tried to continue eating his food, but the insinuation that he was not working toward finishing his degree pissed him off.

There was brief silence before Rodney looked at Kyle before looking at his dad. "I appreciate your hospitality and shit, but why is it that I feel like you are looking down on me. Huh? God didn't make a mistake with me, but I feel like you want me to explain myself to you like I fucked up or something. Nah bruh ... nah." Kyle grabbed his friend and walked him outside leaving Ms. Scott angry, Mr. Scott in shock, and Jasper sitting at the table speechless. Once outside, Rodney told Kyle, "Now, I see what you were talking about . . . that dude always butting in your life and shit! What the hell he mean 'I don't know too many men who would look me in the eye'? Short muthafucka!!"

Kyle jumped in, "Don't sweat that shit. He still thinks that he is in the military. Still bossing people around. I'll talk to him. I gotta talk to him anyway about some shit."

Rodney calmed down after a few minutes and started to head back inside. Kyle called back to him, "Where are you going?"

Rodney didn't even turn around when he said, "I'm about to go back inside and finish eating. Fuuuck that!!" He did just that without saying another word. The Scott's didn't know what to expect after that. Jasper continued eating and smiling the whole time at the awkwardness that was written on their faces as Rodney walked in as if nothing happened only moments earlier. He stifled his laughter as he was thinking to himself that Rodney took it easy on Mr. Scott because he would have normally been more volatile.

Chapter 20

Early the following Monday morning, Kyle, Rodney, and Jasper went to eat breakfast at the Waffle House before departing back to the Mid-South. Jasper had fell in love with the Cheesesteak Omelet Platter and wanted to enjoy eating it one more time. Lamari stopped by briefly to say goodbye before he headed to work.

Kyle seemed to be gradually relaxing each day that he was in the United States. Being around all of his friends helped to ease any tension that he brought with him, and it also kept the tensions down between he and his father. He hated to see his boys go, but the obligations in their lives called for them to continue on. Jasper had to get back to work, and Rodney had work, an upcoming gig, and a family to get home to.

They reminisced about the house parties they had back in the day and their time in the Pembrook band. They talked about women, the war, and music. As they ate, they were able to just be themselves.

The memorial for SPC Filner back in Iraq was truly a sad occasion. Not that any of the other memorials weren't as sad, but the number of occurrences was wearing down the morale of the troops and brewing anger. Chaplain Mosley was trying not to become numb to officiating each one that he was called to do. It was his job, and he was a token of strength and hope for those that believed as well as those that didn't. That day was no different.

After opening remarks by the Chaplain, he allowed a few of Filner's friends in the unit to give a few funny stories and perspectives on the kind of friend and Soldier that he was. Sergeant Bays stood up before the Commander of 53rd Field Artillery was to speak and joked about some of the crazy things that Filner said while on a mission or while they smoked near the big rock where they hung out sometimes. In his brief speech, he pulled out the two cigars that was meant for Filner and Kyle to smoke together. "I will make sure that the L-T gets these when he gets back." Upon hearing that, a jolt ran through the Chaplain as he wondered how Kyle would take the bad news when he came back from leave.

LTC Bloomberg stood up last to make a few remarks before the ceremonial playing of the 21-Gun salute followed by melancholy patriotic and gospel songs. His voice didn't have the boom to it that it did at the beginning of the deployment. He tried to sound optimistic about the role of the United States Armed Forces in Iraq and the ultimate sacrifice that some have met in order to uphold that role.

Sergeant Bays stood as the squad leader and conducted a ceremonial roll call. He loudly called out each name of those standing there in which each Soldier replied back with, "Present". The last name called out was that of the deceased Soldier. Tears rolled down the face of Bays, and his voice cracked as he called out, "Filner!" There was no response. "Specialist Filner!" Still no response. "Specialist Jonathon Filner!" No response. "Specialist Jonathon Mark Filner!" Silence loomed except for a few sniffles that were heard. The sergeant called out Filner's name two more times as it is usually done at memorials. His voice was almost a whisper as he tried to hold himself together the last time he called the name.

After the final name calling and silent response, someone from the deployed element of the Fort Stewart Band commenced with the playing of "Taps". The bugle wailed on slowly as all the Servicemembers stood at attention and rendered a final salute. A big printed, framed picture of Specialist Filner with his big, bright smile stared back at the audience. Knees buckling with slumped shoulders, Sergeant Bays cried audibly, no longer able to keep his composure as he held his salute. The unit commander jumped out of his chair and consoled Bays.

Every commander takes losing one of his/her soldiers hard. Even when it is not their fault. After each of the memorials for one lost from 53rd Field Artillery, Chaplain Mosley allowed the commander to stop by his trailer to share his feelings or just talk. It was especially needed after SPC Filner's memorial. They made small talk before discussing the events of the day. With tears on each of their faces, the two grown men embraced briefly before purge their feelings. At the conclusion of their session, LTC Bloomberg shook the Chaplain's hand and asked him, "Thanks Mosley. Can we pray before I go?"

Kyle was allowed to decompress with his friends and girlfriend before spending the rest of his vacation with his family. His mother wanted to travel somewhere and get out of Georgia, but they couldn't agree on where. They settled with doing some local activities and relaxing at home. Mr. Scott only had one meeting during the time Kyle was home. His mother wanted to do some volunteer work with her sorority sisters, but she was going to play it by ear when the time came.

The tension between Kyle and his father built up after his friends left, as he expected. Kyle's friends being around made Mr. Scott more easygoing and kept his tendency to butt in, especially about military subjects, at bay. Ms. Scott did a wonderful job at crushing any potential flare-ups while they were watching TV together, grocery shopping, out to dinner, or basically any time that she was around them.

Knowing that she wouldn't be there every moment while Kyle was at home, she purposely instigated a conversation with Kyle in a much more approachable manner than her husband. His father tried for the past couple of days and had gotten nowhere. Ever since he was a boy, Kyle was always more prone to share his thoughts with her.

On that particular day, Kyle had just finished talking to Raven on the phone in his room. Once Kyle hung up, Ms. Scott knocked on his door. She hovered in the hallway and waited for an opportunity to take advantage of her husband's absence. He left the house for a couple hours to run some errands.

After placing a pillow in his lap to cover himself after some stirring sexual shit-talking, he said, "Come in." He was relieved to see that it was his mom and she could tell by how he relaxed upon seeing her. "What's up, mom?" Just as she had a good read of her son, Kyle could always tell when his mom was about to divulge something.

She sat down in his chair wasted no time getting to the purpose of why she was in there. "Listen Kyle...I don't know why you and your dad can't get it together, but I don't like being in the middle of it. Two grown ass men shouldn't act like that. Y'all are too much alike." By hearing his mom say a curse word, he knew that she was serious. "I just want to enjoy my son . . . that's all . . . without all that mess you and your dad have going."

"Mom. I'm good. I can't speak for that grown man, but I am ok. You know how he is . . . you married him."

Before he could continue, his mother stopped him, "Watch it!"

Kyle sighed and apologized, "My bad, mom. He just keep rubbing it in my face that he is in charge or knows everything or some shi- stuff. Look at how he was talking to Rodney."

Kyle was visibly getting angry but was trying to keep it cool in front of his mother. "And why did you let him put that note in with your letter to my girlfriend? Talking like he was doing me a favor."

Confused, his mother lost her train of thought, and came back with, "Wh-what? What are you talking about?"

Already on a roll, Kyle continued, "I also found out that he keeps calling LTC Bloomberg in Iraq to check up on me like I am in kindergarten. The whole time that I have been here, dad kept bringing up how much he paid for the hotel room, so I gave him his fu-, I mean, I gave him his money back. And he took it!"

His mother's face looked miserable, yet sweet at the same time. She didn't understand the forcefulness that her husband exhibited when it came to Kyle. He was a great child and grew up to be a model adult. She knew that her husband was proud of their son, but he kept pushing him to be better. She was fearful that Kyle would withdraw if he wasn't allowed to be his own man. He needed to make his own mistakes and to try to carve out his own existence without the fear of not living up to his father's vision of who he thought he should be.

"Kyle do this. Kyle don't do that." Kyle's voice was starting to shake. "I made good grades and shit. I never went to jail. I don't fucking understand." He was never one to really curse in front of his mother, so Brenda Scott clearly knew that her son was really upset. She would normally comment when the curse words started to fly, but she allowed him to get out whatever had been torturing him. "See mom . . . something is wrong with that guy. I don't know what I did to him, but . . .,"

Ms. Scott had heard enough, "Ok. I get your point. Your father loves you and is very proud of you. He just wants the best for you. That's all." Kyle unknowingly rolled his eyes. She continued, "I have talked to him, and I will again. Ever since you were fifteen, you guys have been at each other's throats. I'm sick and tired of it. You can't even get along for a week without some clash." She felt herself about to cry. "I'm not fussing at you, baby. I just wanted for once, to have my two gentlemen act like they are not . . .," her voice trailed off.

Kyle saw the pain in her eyes. Too many years, she was quiet as the relationship between her husband and her son became what it currently was. Kyle went back and forth between trying to win his father's acceptance to not caring whether he was accepted by him or not. His dad pushed Kyle too far out of fear that the changing world was too much for the reserved little boy. His dad thought that Kyle was not tough enough for racism, trials and tribulations that he once had to endure during childhood and his time in the military. His dad realized his faults and often tried to make up for them by using money and whatever military influence that he had left.

"Ok. Mom, I get it. I didn't mean to make you cry. I just wanted to have a good time with my boys, but dad obviously has not changed his overbearing ways. I will try to tolerate him for the little bit of time that I have left here, but warn him not to judge Raven and my friends. And I don't need him calling my unit anymore. You know, Jasper can just drink and talk to his dad without awkwardness. I want to be able to do the same with mine."

His mother dried her tears and forced a smile. "Ok, baby, I will talk to him. Just try to be patient with him. He means well. Ok? He keep acting up, and Ima cut off the cookie factory for a while."

Kyle looked up at his mom, finally smiling, and said, "Ewww, I hate it when you and dad talk like that. I mean, we know that our parents have sex, but we don't need to know that our parents have sex."

The mother and son both laughed and hugged. They remained in the room for a while talking about Iraq, Raven, and Mia. They talked about Mia more than what Kyle wanted to.

The mother and son were not aware that Mr. Scott was at home and had heard the last part of their conversation. He never saw himself as being pushy or butting in too much. He only wanted the best for his only son. He lived away from Kyle and his mother for long periods at a time because he put his career before them inadvertently. He was so focused on knocking down those closed doors of opportunity and wanted to redefine the negative images that some had in a mostly White Army of Black Soldiers and officers.

It took a while for Kyle's dad to come around that afternoon, but decided to do what he heard him say earlier. Since Kyle liked Crown Royal, Mr. Scott stepped out and came home with a nice-sized bottle and various chasers. He also grabbed some wings from one of the local joints and two cigars. He recalled hearing that his son occasionally partook in smoking with some of the Soldiers in his unit. He thought that he could use a similar gesture and have a long overdue discussion with his son.

"Kyle, come join me for a few minutes in my TV room." Mr. Scott took a lot of pride in the den and extra bedroom that he converted into his man cave. Minutes later, Kyle begrudgingly trotted down the stairs into the back of the house. His dad was waiting with a couple of trays in which both had a plate and a glass with ice. The wings and liquor sat on a separate cherry wood table near the leather recliner sofa. The walls were filled with awards from his father's distinguished service in the Army as well as fraternity awards and paraphernalia.

Upon seeing the setup, Kyle felt that his mom had made his dad do all of that as a peace offering. "What's up with all of this, dad?" Still suspicious, he grabbed four wings and poured himself some Crown Royal and ginger ale. Without the usual bravado that he was known for, Mr. Scott humbled himself and kept it straight with his son.

"Listen Kyle. I am glad that you are home. I was worried sick the whole time that you were over there. Hell, ever since you got orders." He took a large swig of his drink before continuing, "I'm not going to lie, son. You see, it's just that . . . well." He took another swig and finally got out his thoughts. "I overheard part of your conversation with your mom. I didn't know that you felt like I was being overbearing." Kyle kept eating his wings and trying not to look at his dad.

After a couple of tense moments, Mr. Scott made them both another drink and kept talking. "Son, I promised myself that I would make you a better man than me. I made so many mistakes, but I was blessed to have strong parents and a wonderful wife to help me back on my path. Then you came along. Then I became the best me that I could so that you wouldn't have to make the same mistakes that I made. So I was wrong to write that note to Raven or talk about your friends like that, but I know that you can be so great with the right people around you."

"Dad, Raven is my girlfriend and my friends have never done me wrong. I don't need you to vet them for me." Kyle popped up to get some more wings and top his drink off. "You know that I don't deal with bustas and crazy chicks. You gotta let me do me." Mr. Scott fought the urge to reply and try to explain his point of view, but his wife did make the "cookie factory" threat. He kept his mouth filled with liquor to keep the words inside that he wanted to say.

After a few more minutes of true confessions along with the liquor, the long-held tension started to ease. After the wings were gone and the bottle was half-empty, the two Scott men were talking and cursing like two old friends. They talked about some of Kyle's exploits in college and Raven. They talked about CPT Cueva and various frat brothers. They talked about music, old and new school. Ms. Scott walked down the stairs to eavesdrop. It warmed her heart to hear her two men enjoying themselves, but she didn't want to listen to their conversations and some of the subjects that they were talking about. She retreated back upstairs thinking about the "cookie" that she was going to give her tipsy husband later.

Chapter 21

Kyle's trip back to the Iraqi theater was uneventful for the most part. Since he started off in Austin, he had to fly back there from Georgia to start his official trek back. Raven was unable to drive down due to her obligations at Fort Hood. He thought that it would have been nice to see her again even if it was only during his 4-hour layover. He spent most of the time sleeping during each flight and reading magazines.

There was a sense of dread and a heavy feeling in his stomach the closer he got to Iraq. His vacation was definitely over, and his nerves confirmed that. He had to get his mind right because he was about to be walking through desert sand, carrying his M-16 rifle everywhere, conducting multiple intelligence assessments, and sitting through meetings from sunrise to sunset again. His sense of awareness naturally heightened to notice things happening around him. He had been so relaxed while at home that the change in awareness made him nervous.

During the flight, he also had a lot of time to reflect on things. He thought about the new memories that he made with his friends and family, as well as Raven. He had garnered a new respect for some of the luxuries that he missed while being overseas. His faith had been strengthened, and he felt that he was going to go back to Iraq with more focus to do his job the best way that he could.

He was glad that he and his dad talked toward the end of his trip. Kyle was just hoping that he would uphold his part of the bargain and back off enough to let him be himself. He respected the man and didn't want to disappoint him, but he also didn't want to be a continuation of his father's military service.

He replayed some of the events that happened during his leave. Overall, it was a great trip. He was glad that all of his boys got along. His ex-fling Brianna blew his phone up, but he wasn't even tempted to go see her. He gained a few pounds with all of the eating and drinking that he did.

As he replayed Mia's actions in his head, he laughed quietly. He saw how Rodney avoided her at first when she got there after being constantly undressed mentally by her. Greg was still unsuccessful at chasing her. She boldly commanded attention from the fellas whenever she felt that no one was talking to her. The most bizarre moment occurred when Mia, tipsy and horny, tried to kiss him.

She had the audacity to try to force herself into his mind and heart a second time before he redeployed. She had stopped by the house the day before he left. After some brief talk, she nervously pushed her large frame against him and told him, "You need a little bit of this before you leave to hold you over until you get back." Kyle was shocked at her boldness after the previous rejection in the hotel parking lot and stiffened his arms again to hold her back. She persisted, and Kyle had to turn her down despite how good she was looking and smelling. She settled for a kiss on the cheek and sat down with her feelings slightly hurt again.

Attempting some type of conciliation prize to spare Mia's feeling while getting a selfish grope in, Kyle walked over to Mia again, asked her to stand up, and hugged her tightly. He whispered in her ear, "If things were different…if things were different." He then slapped her on the booty and held on for a few seconds. Mia jumped in shocked, but she didn't get her hopes up for something more. She did, much to Kyle's surprise, return a slap on his butt and whispered, "Watch out now, Soldier boy. Slaps like that usually come with some dick. This will be here for you if she ever fucks up."

Kyle's boss, CPT Cueva, grabbed one of his drivers and arrived to pick him up shortly after the plane landed. A few others were picked up as well while the majority were waiting on the bus to take them to the designated pickup location. At first, Kyle thought that his boss was being kind to pick up his Soldier. He quickly found out that he was wrong.

"Lieutenant Scott, welcome back. We have a lot of work to do. When you get settled, change clothes and come to the operations center." CPT Cueva said all that before asking how his trip was or if he was hungry or tired. Kyle looked at his watch and saw that it was around 6 p.m. If it was a normal working day, he would have been off duty or close to leaving. He became instantly frustrated because he hadn't had his feet on Iraqi soil for more than 30 minutes.

He looked out of the window and half-heartedly replied with, "Yes sir." Just to emphasize his frustration and drop a hint, Kyle said after a minute, "Sir, do I have time to take a shower?"

CPT Cueva didn't even catch the somewhat sarcastic statement and said, "Sure. Ok, but don't take too long. We really need you."

Kyle was perplexed about what could have been so important that the Captain didn't handle for the three weeks while he was traveling and on vacation. They rode in silence for the rest of the way with Kyle spinning in his thoughts and reacquainting himself to the smell of Iraqi dust and occasional whiffs of sewage on the FOB.

Ten minutes later, Kyle exited the vehicle, grabbed his gear, and headed toward his trailer. *Damn it! I just got off of that long ass flight, and he only picked me up just to put me to work. Really? What is up with that guy?* He grabbed a clean uniform and threw it on the bed. He took off the jeans and button-down shirt that he was wearing and put on his physical training outfit to wear to the shower area. *Fuck that. I'm going to get something to eat too. I'm taking my time.*

After a lukewarm shower, changing into his uniform, and pussyfooting around his room, he deliberately took his time and caught the tail end of dinnertime at the chow hall. He then slowly walked to his office with his to-go plate. He opened the door and gave an exaggerated yawn on purpose. He located CPT Cueva and coolly said, "Whatcha got, sir?"

Kyle's supervisor turned around, looked at his watch, looked at Kyle again, and then back at his watch "Where were you? We got some Intel estimates that need to be updated and ready to brief by zero–eight hundred in the morning. I need you to go through the human intelligence databases and cross examine them against the updated battle trends against this list of adversaries." He then pointed to a list taped on the whiteboard above his head. Without another word, he turned his back to his subordinate and continued typing on his computer.

Frustrated, Kyle sighed and walked over to his desk. He yawned again and started eating the cheeseburger, cookies, and salad in his to-go plate. To prevent his Captain from saying something else, he opened his laptop up, started a blank document, and opened up one of the known adversary databases. He had no intent on starting before he finished eating. *Fucker see me yawing and shit. He can do this shit.*

He had planned on stopping by to see Chaplain Mosley to recap his trip, take a shower, and then go to bed. He didn't know what time he was going to get to bed and was pissed. It would take him a while to catch up on the events that transpired while he was gone before he could even begin guessing what he should put in the estimate.

Half an hour later, Kyle was still yawning and reading through old threat reports when LTC Bloomberg walked in. "LT Scott, what in the world are you doing here? I thought that you were still on rest and relaxation leave."

Kyle stood up and was rubbing his eyes when he replied to his senior supervisor's question. "Sir, I just got back about an hour or so ago. I am working on the Intel estimates that you need in the morning."

Looking perplexed after seeing how tired he was, LTC Bloomberg announced, "Ok L-T. Work on it for about twenty more minutes, give me what you got, and go to bed. Hell, you have been flying and traveling for the past couple of days. You need your rest."

CPT Cueva stiffened upon hearing what his boss said. After the Lieutenant Colonel left, Kyle's boss walked over to him and said, "Looks like the boss man saved you this time. Give me what you got in 15 minutes so I can look over it." He frowned and continued, ". . . then go to bed." Kyle yawned again in agreeance and worked exactly another 15 minutes before submitting his progress and leaving.

The next day, Kyle caught Chaplain Mosley for a few minutes after the morning meeting, called the "Daily Huddle". "Wassup there, K. Scott? How was your leave, man?" Kyle shook hands with the good reverend and smiled.

"It was great, sir! I almost didn't come back." Both gentlemen laughed.

"I understand, K. Scott. I understand."

CPT Cueva was hovering after the meeting as if he needed to talk to Kyle, so the Chaplain told him, "Come talk to me when you get a chance. I don't have anything to do until noon."

Seeing his boss get more and more agitated, he walked away and said to his friend, "Ok, I will stop by your office when I can."

CPT Cueva was still a little upset by being undermined by his superior the night prior by releasing Kyle to get some sleep. He had to take the Intel estimate that was given to him and rework a couple of sections after it was disapproved by the boss. The Captain knew that Kyle wasn't up to speed on latest events in the part of Iraq that his unit was in, but felt overwhelmed and wanted to utilize his lieutenant.

As he talked to Kyle, it was apparent that he still had an attitude. "Lieutenant Scott, what you started last night was pretty decent, but I need you to take this updated copy and refine it. Let me know when you finish." He looked like he really wanted Kyle to disobey or to say something smart back to him.

Kyle metaphorically bit his tongue when he responded, "Sir, did the boss see this? What was his guidance?" Kyle made it up in his mind that he was going to ask the commander himself, but he wanted to afford the opportunity for his supervisor to give some input first so he didn't overstep him. "What parts would you like me to refine?"

The Captain raised his voice, "Hell, do the whole thing over! Focus on the trends of IEDs that have been found or have blown up on the routes that our unit travels. You got that?"

Kyle listened while looking CPT Cueva in the eyes. He remembered what his dad told him often. As a man and an officer, *"You always look them in the eyes. Never back down. You are a man first."*

Not understanding why so much anger was seething from the man in front of him, Kyle just said, "Ok. Yes sir."

He walked away and got started. First, he reviewed the changes from the work that he did the night prior. He disagreed with the changes and highlighted them to check later. He opened up various databases and started his research. While looking at the trends of attacks in the area of operations in which his unit had purview of, he noticed a small blurb about a mortar attack that was on the base days earlier. He copied the information and put it in an empty document to review later.

After about an hour or so, Kyle's eyes started to hurt, so he took that opportunity to go see the Chaplain. He put on his gear, grabbed his weapon, and walked to his trailer. One half was his living quarters, and the other half was his office. Kyle knocked on the door and listened out for the country drawl laced response from the Chaplain.

"Come in, young lieutenant."

Kyle was happy to have a moment to speak with his friend and mentor. When Kyle entered, the Chaplain immediately asked Kyle to take a seat. He didn't return Kyle's enthusiasm, which made Kyle stop smiling.

"Listen, L-T. There was an incident at the area where you smoke and joke with some of the guys. A couple of the guys were slightly hurt, but Specialist Filner didn't make it. His memorial was held Tuesday."

Kyle instantly was flooded with painful guilt and sadness. He had chosen the location because it was far away from the other buildings. At that moment, he was feeling responsible for Specialist Filner's death and the injuries of the others that sustained them. "Sir, no. I mean, no. How?"

Chaplain Mosley walked over and placed his hand on Kyle's shoulder. "Kyle, we are not sure who did it yet, but the guys are asking questions when they go on patrol."

Kyle didn't halfway hear what his friend was saying because he was lost in his own torment. Visions of Filner laughing kept popping in his mind. He recalled the time that Filner almost fought one of the other Soldiers when the joking went too far. He remembered what Filner said was going to be the first thing that he was going to eat with a six-pack of Budweiser beer, two Big Macs and a large order of McDonald's French fries. He was still in disbelief and wanted to cry, but the tears didn't come. He sat there in the chaplain's office, frozen.

"K. Scott? Kyle? Kyle!"

Kyle finally looked back up to see the sincere face of his friend that then looked equally pained.

"It wasn't your fault. You, on your own, gave those Soldiers an escape every week. As young as you are, you were a counselor, a friend, and a kind spirit in this place of craziness. What happened was not your fault. You have to believe me."

Kyle looked down at his hands and saw that they were shaking. The tears still wouldn't come. He kept shaking his head and saying "No" repeatedly. He recollected the report that he had read earlier about the attack on the FOB, and the tears that Kyle wanted to come were replaced by anger. He abruptly felt the need to run back to his office and try to search through the reports until he found out who, or what terrorist sect, most likely orchestrated the attack.

The Chaplain stopped him and advised, "K. Scott, stay here for a few seconds and tell me about Raven." He knew how his battle buddy felt about his girl at home and used that as a point to deflect the feelings going on in his head.

The tactic worked as Kyle instantaneously blurted, "She's great, sir. I enjoyed hanging out with her and *hanging* with her…if you know what I mean. We stayed naked, sir. I mean, it was wonderful getting a chance to see her place and just being there with her." Some of the anger eased as he spoke.

Chaplain Mosley asked about his trip to Georgia as well. Kyle told him about Mia, his father, and getting to see his homeboys.

"It was me, Mia, Greg, Lamari, and the other 'Men of 1302' hanging out in the suite…."

The chaplain cut in and asked, "Who are the 'Men of 1302'?"

Kyle almost snorted at the way his buddy asked him the question. "In college, sir, my roommates that I told you about, Rodney, Jasper, and I used to call ourselves that. The 13-O-2 is the house number where we used to stay."

The two men talked for about an hour. Kyle gave more details of his trip, and the Chaplain told stories about what he did when he went on his leave. Near noon, Chaplain Mosley hopped up, "I hate to cut his short, but I gotta meet some Soldiers at the chapel." Kyle felt better, then he remembered that he had to go back to the office to deal with CPT Cueva.

As expected, CPT Cueva jumped up as soon as Kyle entered the office. "Where were you?"

Kyle, not in the mood after hearing about Filner, almost shouted back, "Sir, I was feeling sick. I was in the bathroom for a while."

CPT Cueva was unable to prove otherwise, so he retorted back, "Where are you with the estimate? Are you done yet?"

Keeping the lies rolling, Kyle tap danced around another response, "Sir, I am about done with what you asked for, and I can have it to you shortly. Actually, I can send you something after your meeting at 1300."

Kyle wasn't going to change much, but he planned on looking more in the mortar attack that killed Specialist Filner. After he completed his directed duties, he did just that. He read the official reports, the eyewitness statement from Sergeant Bays, and reviewed the projectile analysis. He looked at recently captured terrorists and tried to cross-reference their whereabouts with the patrol reports. He barely looked away from his computer screen since he was imbued with a renewed focus. He held back tears a couple of times as he read report after report and thought about what it must have been like that night for Filner and the others. He couldn't shake the feeling that he was responsible. Finding the perpetrators of the attack was his only way to redeem himself.

He stayed later than usual that day. As he was heading out of the door, tired mentally and physically, he heard Sergeant First Class Daphne Carson call his name. She was the senior enlisted in the personnel actions staff office.

"Sir, I didn't know that you were back. A letter came in the mail two days ago. Standby, and I will go get it."

Kyle stood there confused because given the time that it took for a letter to come from the states to Iraq was about a good week or so. He had just finished seeing all the people who had written him or who had his address. He assumed it was from his mom's church or something.

Minutes later, SFC Carson returned with his letter. Kyle grabbed it, and told her, "Thank you. You have a good night now."

Upon looking at it, his confusion intensified. He noticed that it was a letter from Raven. *Why would she write me a letter when I just saw her?* He rushed to his room, took off his gear, and sat on the bed to read it. He assumed that the letter would be full of phrases like, "I am glad that I saw you" or "I miss you, baby." He smiled at the thought and opened it.

Halfway through, his smile disappeared and Kyle suddenly felt like he couldn't breathe. He felt dizzy even though he was sitting down. By the time he finished reading it, he was encompassed between the feelings of sheer anger and absolute sadness. He closed his eyes in disbelief and read the letter over again.

Kyle,

I am glad that we had a chance to spend some time together. I missed you...and that dick. Anyway, I really enjoyed you, but I wanted to tell you something. I debated on telling you while you were here. You were so happy, and I didn't want to ruin it. I know it is rough over there for you, but I have to be honest with you.

Baby, I never wanted to hurt you, but I have a confession. Please don't be too mad at me, but I will understand if you never want to talk to me again. Ok. Here it goes . . .

I made a mistake one night. I didn't cheat on you or anything. I was at a party with some of the other lieutenants here, and I kissed someone. Me and this guy were just talking outside and he kissed me. Nothing else happened. I promise.

I thought that it may not be such a big deal, but I know how I would feel if you did that to me. I was missing you, and it just happened. While you are over there, maybe we should not be together and see what's up when you get back. Think about it. We ain't even stationed at the same base. When would I see you? Maybe your dad was right.

Don't be too mad at me. I guess you will stop sending me flowers every month. I did enjoy getting them. You always picked out beautiful tulips and roses. I feel bad, and I was going to wait until you got back to tell you. I just felt too bad. I wrote this letter the same day you left and sent it. I didn't want to ruin your fun with your friends in Georgia and all.

When you stop being mad at me, I will still be here for you if you want to talk. If you don't call, I will understand. Regardless of what you think, I really care about you.

Raven

Kyle stayed on his bunk, his head swimming in utter disbelief. Part of him wanted to actually cry, but he couldn't and wouldn't let that happen. After a few minutes, he said aloud, "What? Kissing is cheating." With no one in the room, he continued his rant, "She just closed the letter with just her name. That is not like her." He thought back over the past conversations with Raven and dissected each one to see what he did wrong. He couldn't think of anything.

Twenty minutes later, he was still sitting on the edge of his bed stricken with fatigue and suddenly heartbroken. The letter had since fell from his hands and onto the dusty floor. He looked for signs if she was unhappy or lonely, and couldn't find any. He felt stupid for being so open and honest with her just to be dumped so easily. He didn't know if he felt more betrayed or if he was just disappointed with Raven.

He contemplated working it out with Raven since it was only a kiss, but Raven's possible emotional tie to the unknown guy was too much to bear at the time. Kyle remembered Jasper's dad saying sometimes around the boys, *"I ain't saying that cheating is ever right, but it is totally different for men than women. You see, men can see a big booty, handle it, and be back in time for dinner. Women though...that's something else. They carefully select while they evaluate you versus the other options.*

*When they choose someone else, they already have fifty lies to
cover it up and at least three friends ready to back up any lie
they haven't even told you yet."* The newly confirmed
truthfulness of the memory made him angry.

Kyle was tempted to run to the internet café to send an
email or over to the phone trailer to call her, but all of the events
of the day were too much. Dealing with a lazy, yet overbearing
boss, learning about the death of Specialist Filner, and then a
"Dear John" letter from a woman that he thought he was falling
in love with brought his energy to an overwhelmingly low level.
He reached for his alarm clock and set it for 6 a.m. He laid
down for the night with the lights on and slept in most of his
uniform. His last thoughts before dozing off was to definitely
cancel the monthly flower delivery to Raven.

Chapter 22

Coping mechanisms are sometimes taught, but each person learns how to cope in ways that best suits them. Kyle was spending extra time in the gym and in the office as his coping mechanisms. After hearing about Filner's death and getting dumped by his girlfriend on the same day, something within him changed. Regardless of the bad news, he was still in a war area and had a job to do. He couldn't let his emotions get the best of him because emotions led to mistakes, and mistakes could lead to more deaths.

Against his better judgement and only increasing his frustration, Kyle tried to contact Raven a couple of times, but there was no answer. There were no replies to his emails as well. He just wanted to hear her say what she was thinking. He felt that it was owed to him…at least. Chaplain Mosley told him that she was probably scared to hear what he had to say and suggested giving her a couple of weeks before reengaging.

His response was, "It is better to know now than to find out when I get back. Fuck that bitch. Ummm, excuse me, sir.

You know what I mean." Kyle ignored the advice and persisted until he was given more of an explanation.

Raven wanted to reach out to Kyle from Texas and reply to him. The anger that he displayed in voicemails and emails cautioned her from responding to him. Kyle's messages were full of accusations which, to Raven, were unfounded and quite harsh. Raven didn't think that it was a big deal that she kissed a guy. She felt terrible for doing so, but she wanted to be sure that she wasn't rushing into something long-term before a proper foundation had been set. It was hard to have a long distance relationship with someone in the United States, let alone with someone who lived on the other side of the world.

Overly logical people, like Kyle, weren't the same as typically emotional people; therefore, the anger of overly logical people was different as well. Kyle kept playing their relationship over in his mind for any clue to what he did wrong or if he did anything wrong at all. He had shared so much with her and couldn't grasp what would compel Raven to put herself in a scenario where she would be tempted to kiss another guy. Kyle's thoughts ran away, and he saw Raven doing much more than having a kiss. He felt stupid now for trusting her and starting to love her. Maybe his father was right about Soldiers getting caught up before and during deployments. Kyle felt like he was one of them.

Kyle's body was benefiting from the extra attention that he paid to it as he dealt with his love frustration with extra bench presses, barbell curls, and several minutes on the treadmill. CPT Cueva was benefiting with the extra work that he didn't have to tell Kyle to do. Through it all, Kyle's mind and heart were suffering.

Chaplain Mosley was worried about his friend. It wasn't the first "Dear John" letter scenario that he had provided counseling for, but Kyle was taking it harder than he expected. He seemed to be distracted sometimes as they were talking about various things. Other times, he was more quiet than usual. Chaplain Mosley offered kind words occasionally, but he knew that only time would heal the hurt that the young lieutenant was feeling.

"It is these times that you must come together in your units, your squads... your teams and lean on the Lord. Amen. Some of you have seen death, some have seen combat, and some... have seen the enemy face-to-face....right...outside...of...those barriers."

The congregation erupted with "Amen!", "Alright now!" and "Yessir!"

"I am here to tell ya THAT is not the only enemy that you have to contend with."

Chaplain Mosley always had a full house, but the war helped many more find their way to the local chapel, especially when he was leading the service. He was in the midst of his sermon when LTC Bloomberg walked into the chapel. He took a seat in the back and attempted to remain unnoticed, but Kyle and some others saw him.

Continuing to stir the crowd, Chaplain Mosley was on a roll and had sweat, mostly from excitement mixed with the Iraqi heat, falling from his shiny bald head. "See...now. My brothers and sisters....God won't take away your faith. A huh....the enemy...the terrorists can't take your faith. Follow me now.... Only you..." He received a few laughs when he said, "Somebody is going to be mad at me before I finish," then he continued, "Only you can take away your faith."

Kyle was attentive as he heard his friend say, "Corinthians 5:7 says, some of y'all know it, 'For we live by faith, not by sight.' Now....what does that mean? Huh? Nah nah nah, I'll give you another one. Write this one down now." Chaplain Mosley took a deep breath and started back with another faith-related Bible verse, "Matthew 21:21 says 'Jesus replied, "I tell you the truth, if you have faith and DO...NOT...DOUBT, not only can you do….'. Now….I'ma stop right there. Oh, there is more, but right now…someone…needed to hear…just…THAT…part!"

Several people shouted "Amen" just then Kyle happened to look toward LTC Bloomberg who seemed enthralled by what was just said. "I'm talking to ya…*and* about ya. Somebody doesn't hear me! I'm talking to ya…*and*…about ya. Can I get an Amen up in here?"

Once the sermon was over, Kyle headed back to his trailer to reflect and catch a quick nap before returning to work. He knew better than to hang around after the service for his chaplain buddy was often inundated by worshippers that wanted to shake his hand or say a few words.

In his trailer, Kyle sat on the bed and thought about his nightmares, Raven, and Specialist Filner. He couldn't let those events shake his faith. They almost did. He doubted that Chaplain Mosley tailored that sermon just for him, but he felt that he was definitely one of those than needed to hear it that day.

Kyle had been back in Iraq for a few weeks now since his vacation. Life had returned to normal for all of his friends for the most part. Raven on the other hand had been going through a small turmoil back at Fort Hood. Work was as stressful as expected for a young lieutenant, and she tried to get over Kyle. She tried to act as if her relationship with him never existed.

Partially out of guilt and partially out of Kyle's persistence to get an explanation, she accepted one of his phone calls. The first few minutes were mostly silence and very few words as they both didn't know what to say as they finally spoke. Eventually, Kyle jumped into his accusatory tone and spewed remarks about his disappointment in her and his faithfulness. She desperately tried to get in a few words, but he kept badgering her with questions, sarcasm, and accusations.

After a few minutes of hearing Kyle verbally beat her up, she had had enough. She awoke from a restful sleep to answer the call from him and sat in her bed with a fast beating heart and tears moistening her face. Kyle broke his rant and asked her, "So what do you have to say?"

She actually pulled the phone away from her face and grimaced at the phone as if Kyle could see the attitude printed on her face. She wanted to say all that was flowing in her head, but she only managed to scream, "I'm sorry. Shit!!!" She hung up the phone not wanting to hear anymore and laid back down attempting to go to sleep.

After the argument with Kyle that morning, in her time zone, she decided to spitefully give the guy that she had kissed a chance. She knew it was only a matter of time before she crossed paths with him again, and she was right in that he would try again to push up on her. Two days later, they were both at a happy hour event. She wrote her number down on a napkin and placed it in his hand before she left.

When he called, she agreed to let him take her out to dinner which turned out to be quite uneventful. Captain Chris Tomlinson, the guy that kissed Raven, seemed to lack conversation other than his favorite sexual positions and inquiring about which positions she liked.

That turned out to be the culminating event in which she realized how much she messed up. Kyle discussed random facts, was in tune with his insecurities, and gave her nothing but affection despite his hard exterior. Chris was near her, and it was convenient, but her lukewarm attraction to him mostly centered on that fact alone.

Days after the awful dinner date, she felt physically sick after moping around distraught about the great guy that she lost and was disappointed that being lonely was her weakness. She felt that another apology wouldn't do. The emails that she wanted to send probably wouldn't be replied to since she had not replied to his previous ones. It was only when he stopped sending emails that she started to look forward to getting the next one. In an attempt to get herself back together, she pulled out a few sheets of notebook paper and started to write a letter.

The following Tuesday, Kyle was in the gym that he routinely frequented to get in a quick thirty minute or so workout. He worked on his biceps and back muscles on Tuesdays. He had to wait longer than normal to share the weights and benches that he needed because more people were in there at the time.

Frustrated with those who wasted time and talked instead of working out, he allowed his stream of consciousness to flow wherever his thoughts carried him. Lost in his thoughts, he felt like he was being watched. Lo and behold, he caught SSG Melanie Sheffield blatantly staring at him as she was riding one of the stationary bikes. He tried to play it off like he didn't see her, but he was drawn in by the intensity of her stare. She didn't care who saw her.

Just being playful, Kyle winked at her and walked toward the dumbbell rack. When he finished a set of bicep curls, he looked back in the staff sergeant's direction and saw her wink back. Nervously, Kyle looked around to see if anyone saw it, but no one seemed to be paying attention. Kyle playfully winked again. In response, she bit her bottom lip and winked back. He chuckled to himself and finished his workout. As vulnerable as he felt, the last thing he needed was to get caught up with an enlisted Soldier. Since it was not allowed for enlisted Soldiers and officers to fraternize, he kept any urge to do anything more with the beautiful woman, who looked tempting while she exercised, to himself.

Twenty minutes later, Kyle finished his workout and grabbed a bottle of water from the large stack in one of the corners. He walked out of the small, climate-controlled gym and headed toward his part of the FOB where he worked and slept. He took fifteen or so steps before SSG Sheffield boldly ran up to him and said, "Sir, I may be wrong, but I would say that you were flirting with me."

Kyle's heart started to pump fast with fear that maybe winking twice would be the start of an investigation. Instead, the winking gave SSG Sheffield the confidence to approach the young lieutenant who she had been curious about for some time. She was just as nervous to take a chance at something forbidden that could possibly be remarkable. To her, Kyle seemed "squared away", or had everything put together well both physically and professionally, as Soldiers would say. He also seemed like he would keep his mouth shut if something was to transpire between them. She was hoping that she was right.

Kyle was dumbfounded as he looked around to see if anyone was watching.

She chimed in, "Look sir...ummm. I am not trying to get you in trouble but I saw you one day and knew that I had to say something to you." Kyle really liked her accent, and it made her words sound sexier than they were meant to be. "It's cool if you don't want to hang out, with you being an officer and all, but I promise no one will know if you don't tell anybody."

Feeling a combination of vulnerable, nervous, and horny, he whispered to the staff sergeant, "Sure. We can talk, but we have to play it cool. There are too many nosey people around. You feel me?" Kyle was shocked that those words even came out of his mouth. He was always one to follow the rules, but the Raven incident might have weakened him to such temptation.

They casually spoke for a few minutes, but quickly changed the subject to exercise routines when anyone walked by them. They agreed to find a way to meet up that wouldn't bring too much attention to them. There was no rule to stop officers and enlisted Soldiers from being friends, but it would be suspicious if two young single people were suddenly too chummy, regardless of their rank. They agreed that the gym would be their spot to link up and meet. If both were there at the agreed time, they would find a way to get some conversation in without attracting too much attention.

After an awkward silence, they said their goodbyes and walked away in different directions. Neither one of them looked back. SSG Sheffield was overjoyed and felt that her prayers had been answered. She wanted a decent man in her life. She was not dissuaded by Kyle's rank because she thought about getting out of the military anyway. Kyle, on the other hand, was torn between right and wrong. He was going to play it low-key and let her make all of the moves. He also played scenarios in his head about how he could see her without her uniform or workout clothes and not get caught.

Chapter 23

Two weeks had gone by, and Kyle was no closer to finding those responsible for Filner's death. He spent more time at work looking for tie-ins as new intelligence reports came in, which meant spending more time around CPT Cueva. There was undeniably a growing tension between him and his superior officer. They would sometimes get into debates about the enemy trends that were reported in their area of operations among other things. Kyle always stayed professional even though his boss would throw him insults like, "Blockhead" and "Bumbling Idiot".

CPT Cueva grew increasingly irritable as the deployment lingered. Pretty much a loner, he didn't have the same outlets that Kyle and some of the other staff had. CPT Cueva really had no one to vent to during dinner or between meetings. He had no one to call back in the states to give him a supportive word every so often. All he had was his job, which he hated that most of the time. He would spend many late nights looking at photos, tagging confiscated weapons, and writing reports that no one read.

At each morning meeting, he would begin by giving a weather report. Even though providing the weather was typical staff practice for an intelligence officer in a tactical unit, his peers oddly nicknamed him "Weatherman". He despised it immensely and was very vocal about it, but some still joked regardless. With no proper outlet, he took out his frustrations and insecurities on those who worked for him.

Kyle, on the contrary, had multiple outlets including his buddy Chaplain Mosley, his gym time, and more recently, SSG Sheffield. She and Kyle met up every so often to engage in small talk. They were always stealthy about it. They would talk at the gym sometimes when not many people were around. They would meet up on the more deserted side of the FOB when they could both get away and wore their PT uniforms to minimize attention. Slowly, she had become what Raven once was – the voice that told him everything would be ok when he complained about work and his boss.

Kyle and Melanie enjoyed the times that they were able to hang out, and the secrecy made it more exciting. Her New York accent and bronze skin were alluring, but the fear of creating a scenario that could end his career kept him in check. There was no way to guarantee that she would keep things in check if their lips or bodies ever touched. He thought about it constantly and considered taking a chance. In their conversations, Kyle learned that she was a single mother who ended an engagement to another staff sergeant two years prior. Upon hearing that, he thought about something his dad said to some of his Army buddies once about getting with women who were enlisted. "See, if you are going to do it, you gotta choose carefully. You got to find you a Sergeant First Class or above, or a Staff Sergeant who is divorced with some kids. That way, they already know the game and have too many years in. They have just as much to lose as you do."

SSG Sheffield didn't exactly fit the description of his dad's words, but she did have a lot to lose to if they were to get caught. Regardless, Kyle couldn't account for her jealous girlfriends or another male Soldier upset that she didn't get with him.

SSG Sheffield was ready for Kyle to make a more aggressive move. Their conversations were enlightening and a breath of fresh air compared to the guys she dated in the past. The confidence he exuded and his deep voice got her going every time. She wasn't going to tell anyone about their meetings at the possible detriment of losing a great guy. She always placed a condom in her pocket when she planned to meet him just in case her yearning would be satisfied. She felt his anxiety but was looking forward to feeling more of him physically.

One time, they met by the large concrete barriers near the maintenance yard for some of the tanks of various units. The yard was controlled by civilian contractors that believed in not working more than 10-hour days. Therefore the area was usually bare of personnel most late nights. Kyle specifically picked the location based on his tactical training. The lighting and position of the barriers allowed him to see or hear anyone coming toward them but kept them concealed from a distance. As long as they weren't too loud, no one would suspect anyone of being there.

They usually talked about their jobs and stuff back in the United States. When both of their forbidden thoughts got the best of them at the same time, there was always a bizarre silence and staring. Kyle usually broke the silence with a question like, "So how's your son doing?" That particular time during the silence, Melanie walked over to Kyle and pressed her chest against his. They were close in height so her lips were about level to his. She patiently waited for the man that she prayed about to claim what they both wanted.

Kyle felt trapped. He was too far in and too much of a man to back away. Her fruity scented body wash was abating any desire for him to actually do so. He couldn't think of a joke or subject to bring up to ease the mood. She blinked slowly, and he leaned in while grabbing her waist. He could feel her heart beating faster than his as they kissed.

Nothing mattered at that moment except the genuine lust that they felt. All the pains of the deployment and the matters that plagued their hearts and minds were replaced by the enjoyment of a forbidden act. They were oblivious to their surroundings as they focused on each other. They groped at each other and Kyle could feel the heat coming from her shorts. She could have easily pulled them down and leaned against one of the barriers that surrounded them. The sudden thought that snapped him back to reality was what could happen not only if he had sex with an enlisted Soldier, but got her pregnant. He pulled back from her embrace.

The cute and appealing staff sergeant was too roped into the moment to mention that she had brought a condom as she reached for Kyle again. Kyle, sensibly and gently, pushed her back saying, "Not here, not now." They kissed once more, but Kyle stopped it when it started to escalate past the previous level. "Let's stop now before we go too far. I mean, let's plan this another way."

Dejected, Melanie nodded her head up and down. They stood in muteness, occasionally smiling at each other as they allowed time for their urges to simmer down. Kyle grabbed himself to adjust his firm penis in his PT shorts. Before they left the area, they agreed that they would go all the way next time and made a plan as to how it would go down.

Rodney had just gotten home from his part time job and was dozing off on the couch when he received a text from his ex-girlfriend, Tasha. The texts had started coming more regularly and was starting to bother him. She knew that he was married but would send the occasional "How are you?" text or one talking about someone she had met during her evolution of becoming an R&B sensation. That day she was sending texts about their past relationship.

Tasha Currin was part of the up and coming group, Onyx Pearl, who was in the midst of recording their debut album. They were finishing up a session, and she had the urge to text her former lover.

Do you miss me?

                           No.

Come on. I miss you.

                          Why?

Why not? I was just thinking about you!

                          So? Are you drunk again?

The last time that Tasha texted Rodney, she was drunk after a party and felt the need to try to explain herself about what happened in college. Too tired to read it or even care, he decided that he was going to cut the texting short that day. As he was typing a message, another one came through.

`You should come out and visit.  You can play your guitar on one of the tracks that the group is recording.`

He erased the text that he was typing and decided to give her a harsh reminder.

`No.  I'm married and not coming to visit.  Remember?`

She sat in the car that was taking her and her group back to their apartment in silence, partly mad and partly sad. She decided to end the text session.

`I remember.`

During the back and forth texting, Katrina walked in after her final class for the day. She shocked him and said, "Hey baby. Who you texting?" Rodney, who was not very good at lying, quickly threw Jasper's name, and reputation, out as a quick cover.

"Oh shit. Ummm, that was Jasper telling me about how he had some girl crying last night after they fucked."

Not wanting to hear another story about Jasper's exploits, Katrina rushed back to her room to change clothes before she picked up their daughter. Relieved that she didn't ask too many more questions, Rodney quickly muted the volume of his phone in case Tasha was going to send more texts. He kicked off his shoes and laid down to catch a few Z's before his daughter arrived home ready to play.

Later that night, Jasper went on an impromptu date. It had been a minute since he actually had a true date. One of the girls that worked in his office building shamelessly asked him what he was doing later after work. Hiding his eagerness, he coolly said, "Let's check out that little bakery on Elvis Presley Boulevard after we get off." She agreed, and they both braved the typical after five Memphis traffic to make it to Mama's Best Sweets and Bakery around seven.

They both ordered something sugary to eat and commenced with some basic first date conversation as they ate. Jasper had seen her around the building, but he thought that she was too stuck up to be approached. The conversation started going well and Jasper was optimistic about a possible new love, until she had a moment of honesty. She had a boyfriend that she was waiting to propose to her, but she wasn't convinced that he would make the move so she was starting her search for a new one.

A slight rage had overcome Jasper as he couldn't believe what he had just heard. He wasn't a saint himself, but he was shocked at the audacity of the woman in front of him. Of course, he was convinced that he could have a chance to play in the pussy of the coworker in front of him, but he wasn't in the mood to be someone's part time while they waited on their full time to act right.

He enjoyed his chocolate cheesecake and came up with the excuse that he had to get home to feed his dog. He didn't have a dog, but it sounded convincing enough for him to exit the scene. With that, he didn't have to try to convince the trifling woman in front of him to give him some draws while she waited on her guy to man up. She didn't feel any guilt when she said to Jasper, "I only give some to my man, but I might make an exception for you."

It took quite an effort for Jasper to not frown after hearing that statement. He took the number and smiled but had no plans on ever using it.

Chapter 24

Kyle saw SSG Sheffield a few times over the next week. Their system worked. If they both showed up in the gym between eight and nine on certain nights, they would make plans to see each other around midnight in their usual spot. Each time, heavy groping and kissing happened before they talked about their jobs and other subjects. Their spirited meets always ended the same – heavier groping and a promise to see each other again.

The second time that they met up that week, they made plans to meet in Kyle's trailer at 2 a.m. Saturday morning. It was less risky to hookup at such a late hour, and their mutual desire justified the risks.

The plan was simple. Melanie, would act like she had to go to the bathroom around the designated time. She would head toward Kyle's room, which was not too far from one of the bathroom trailers. Kyle would set his alarm and unlock his door around the time of her arrival. She was instructed to walk in and lock the door behind her.

Eager, Melanie tossed and turned while checking her watch constantly. She wanted Kyle so badly, and she was anxiously anticipating the experience that was about to occur. She had to combat the recurring thought of what a future would be like with him. Tired of the military life, she was silently hoping that all would work out with the lieutenant who was the object of her newfound affection so she could be an officer's wife after not renewing her enlistment.

Kyle, was just the opposite. He set his alarm to go off at 1:30 am. He wanted to get some rest before handling the thick thighs of the woman coming to his trailer. He was anxious too, but it was more from the fear of getting caught. As the alarm rang, he hopped up and used the bathroom and surveyed the area to make sure people weren't still up and walking around. Observing mostly stillness, he felt a little more at ease and returned to his room. He left the door unlocked.

Twenty minutes after his return, his heart jumped as his door opened. The lights were off, and the only illumination in the room came from his laptop. Without wasting any time, SSG Sheffield took off her PT jacket and shirt and threw them aside. Kyle sat frozen and watched as two perky, beautiful breasts made their way to where he sat. He instantly pulled her down quietly and kissed her neck, her nipples, and her lips. Aware of the need to be as quiet as possible, neither one of them moaned.

They both had condoms ready, but they teased each other a little bit longer as they enjoyed the ability to play without looking over their shoulder every so often. While they rubbed and hugged, kissed and licked, a group of Soldiers returning from a patrol walked past the trailer talking. The noise was enough to make them freeze in the middle of their actions. Both half-naked, they remained still and silent for quite a while.

After a while, Melanie aggressively tried to get things back in the direction that they were going. Kyle couldn't get himself together as the interruption snapped him back to reality. He noticed that he was no longer erect, regardless of how she touched him. He kept thinking about them getting caught eventually, though it was highly unlikely they would have gotten caught that night.

Feeling dejected again, though understanding, she continued to touch his chest and arms more for her enjoyment than to spur arousal. They both knew that the moment was over despite how much they wanted to spin things back up.

After some whispered small talk, Kyle offered, "Mel, how about we kinda chill until we get back? I mean, we are redeploying back to the states soon. We can get together with less fear of this bullshit."

She was ready to curse aloud, but she agreed under the condition that he would at least finger her right then. He agreed and proceeded to do so. He almost got to the point of reengaging some copulation but his sense got the best of him.

After she climaxed, they both held each other and almost dozed off in the blissfulness of the moment. Not to chance them being caught by the pending sunrise, Kyle compassionately ushered her up to get dressed and vacate his trailer. She made it a point for him to get a good view of her bare ass as a sign of what he could've gotten and what is due to come.

Once dressed, they embraced in silence. She focused on how good it felt to be in the presence of a decent guy, while Kyle took in the aroma of whatever shampoo she used. They had a final kiss, and Kyle thought about Raven kissing him like that. Once she left, Kyle realized that his dick was hard again, and he cursed to himself for not being able to seal the deal earlier. He set his alarm clock and grabbed a towel to finish what he had started earlier. He thought of both Raven and Melanie while doing so.

LTC Bloomberg started seeking the counsel of his chaplain more often. Not raised in the church and not much of a religious guy, the notion of seeking prayer and spiritual guidance was still foreign to him. War has a way of toiling a person's spirit though. His time in Iraq was harsher than any combat he had ever seen. He kept up his tough front while in front of his unit, but deep down, he was falling apart. The already broken promise and unfulfilled guarantee of bringing everyone in 53rd Field Artillery back home alive, had him stressed.

Not only was the commander another soul seeking assistance, he was Chaplain Mosley's boss. Therefore the chaplain made time for him whenever he needed to talk. That, and the fact that he saw a strong man about to reach his breaking point, was enough to make him a priority. He offered him opportunities to be vulnerable in a world where he was known for being hard-hitting and a somewhat detached leader.

The prayer requests were more frequent and sometimes came during the morning meetings. The commander would occasionally say something like, "Chap, give us a quick prayer or word of the day or something."

The southern Baptist was always ready to bless the staff with a little something without overly thinking of what to say. The majority of the weary staff soaked up whatever positive anecdotes or sayings that he conveyed.

In an abandoned building partially destroyed by a bombing, a group of the Abna Aleadala, or Sons of Justice sect of Al Qaeda, met to discuss their next move. Motivated by recent successes with the placement of IEDs and other attacks, the group was ready to up the ante with something more daunting.

Abna Aleadala was to planning multiple simultaneous attacks meant to pull attention away from where their main objective was going to take place. Something to be deemed epic was in the works, and Aqeel Abboud was trusted with more responsibility after getting the coordinates for the mortar attack on the nearby Army base. The sect leader told him, "مهنأ نآلا يعرف نوف نأ مهنأ سيلت آمنق. ولا حتى آمن نارو ءارجدران امناوقواعدها" which translated in English to mean, "Now they know that they are not safe. Not even safe behind their walls and their bases."

Feeling that the attack was enough to avenge his father, Aqeel was satisfied. He later realized that he was too deeply involved to walk away without doing more for his sect. The promise of financial gain was tempting to Aqeel, but his fear of being killed for disloyalty and not following orders was greater. Aqeel reported that night and waited for instructions.

Chapter 25

It was Jasper's turn to get a phone call from his homie Kyle as coordinated in an email the week prior. Kyle stated that he had something to tell him. Jasper took a nap earlier that night to prepare for at least a 30-minute phone call in which there was a seven hour time difference between them. The tone of the email made Jasper nervous so he was anxious to hear what Kyle had to say.

When his cell phone finally rang, Jasper jumped up to answer it, "Wassup mane?"

Kyle had the same nervous tone that appeared to be in his email as he replied, "Jasper, how are you?"

Not wanting to waste time, given that it was in the early hours of a work day, Jasper jumped right to it, "So…what's going on, pimp? You ok over there?"

Kyle took a deep breath and began to tell Jasper about his risky rendezvous days earlier with Melanie in his room. Since the phone provided a limited amount of privacy, he spoke in their unique symbolic code and hinted as much as he could.

After many years of friendship, Jasper followed flawlessly as he listened. Eventually, the person in the booth eventually left, so Kyle continued normally in a whispered tone, "My brother, she was right there naked as hell…waiting. You know that I am not a punk with mine, so I was ready to handle it. Then….then…I thought about Raven. I mean, it messed me up…if you know what I mean."

Jasper jumped in, "So your dick wouldn't stay up? I mean, bruh, she was ready for you to slay that thang, and you thought about your ex-girlfriend? Damn." After a moment of silence, he continued, "So you going to get a chance to handle that, bruh? You about to 13-O-2 that thang?"

Kyle laughed at the reference to the phrase they used to use in college referring the attempts they made to damn near turn girls out that came to their house back in the day. He replied to Jasper, "Man, something ain't right about it. Jasper, I don't think that I am over Raven honestly."

Jasper sucked his teeth in response and said, "Mane, you better get over that. Raven cool and all, but that thing is over…unless y'all going to work it out." He continued with a few more comments which went really unheard by Kyle as he felt himself about to push out something painful.

"So Jasper, you saying that I should get over that, huh? Just like you got over Tina?" He didn't know why he was angry, and he actually thought that it was a low blow. Kyle was always known for being blunt.

Hearing Kyle say Tina's name right then forced a standing Jasper to sit down. The truth behind Kyle's statement caused shock and irritation. It forced any reply from Jasper to stay silent. After some quiet awkwardness, Kyle changed the subject and the conversation continued for a few more minutes. The person monitoring the time that each Soldier spends in the booths, walked by and tapped Kyle on the shoulder. It prompted him to wrap up the conversation so the next person could make a call.

Other than being sleepy and frustrated from his talk with Kyle, Jasper had a typical day at work. Their conversation had put some things on his mind that lingered with him throughout the day. His thoughts ranged from *Kyle was right* to *Tina deserves to be in jail* to *Damn, I wished that it would have worked out.*

He thought about it as he drove home in Memphis after-work traffic and as he walked up the stairs to his apartment.

Jasper sat on his couch and sighed. He pulled out a CD that Sonya let him borrow. He had never heard of Eric Roberson before. Jasper had only listened to his CD, *The Esoteric Movement,* a couple of times since he borrowed it. He vaguely recalled one track that would be appropriate for his mood right then. He skipped through the CD until he got to "She Went Away" and placed it on repeat. It was the perfect song as he sat in silence and thought about Tina. He had to get over her just like he told Kyle to get over Raven.

After talking to Jasper the night before, Kyle decided to wait in the long lines at the AT&T phone trailer a second night to call Mia for some additional advisement regarding putting closure on his relationship with Raven. He could pretty much assume what she was going to say, but he still wanted a female perspective anyway. He just hoped that she didn't take the opportunity to put a bid in for herself during their conversation.

Kyle emailed her to tell her that the phone call was coming in order to give her time to go to sleep early or take a nap.

Mia sleepily answered the phone, "Hello."

Kyle took a deep breath and started telling her the reason for his call. He rushed it and kept talking in order to not give Mia a chance to cut in. He talked about whether or not he should call Raven to say how he really felt or was it too much. He asked if it was ok to forgive her and move on. He did not talk about his new friend Melanie.

Mia had originally heard about Kyle's breakup with Raven from Lamari one day while she, Lamari and Greg were having lunch. She yawned a couple of times as she listened to Kyle. When he was finished she said, "Damn. I knew something was wrong with her. She had your nose too wide open and shit." She could damn near tell that Kyle was frowning through the phone, so she toned it down some. "I mean, she probably is a decent person and all, but uh…she still kissed someone else though. That's only what she told you. Shiiit, who knows what else happened."

Kyle remained silent biting his tongue so he wouldn't jump in while she talked. She continued, "Listen, it is understandable for you to hold on a lil longer. Time will heal your heart, Soldier Boy, and you will get another one." She knew her friend well enough to know that a question with a lot of logic and very little emotion was about to come from Kyle. She quickly threw in the conversation, "Seriously, you are a good dude. She will be aight. You need to focus on coming back home alive, Soldier boy."

Just when Kyle thought that Mia wasn't going to put herself into the discussion, she proved him wrong.

"See, I wouldn't have done you like that, but you don't want me though."

Kyle sighed in response and thanked her for the advice. "Well, I know that it is early your time, so I will let you go. Thanks again Mia!" He almost said a friendly "I love you", but he thought that it was not appropriate after what she just said. After a few minutes more of conversation, they hung up. Mia rolled over in her bed as Kyle headed back to his. Mia's last thought before dozing back off for a short nap was, *I might try to give him some when he gets home.*

The next week In Texas, Raven starting unpacking a care package that she was going to send to Kyle. Emotionally, she went from sad to angry then sad to angry again. It had been a while since she'd heard from him. She felt that she was too beautiful and desirous to worry about Kyle's cutting words and over-logical innuendos.

She placed the personal hygiene items in her bathroom and placed the candy and food items in her kitchen. She had a moment of weakness and cried a few tears when she grabbed the bag of pretzels that was in the box. Pretzels were one of Kyle's favorite foods. Instead of keeping them for later consumption or giving them away, she threw the unopened bag into the garbage can.

She also did not receive any response to the letter that she recently wrote. She wasn't expecting one but was really hoping for something considering all of the weeks that had passed. She couldn't understand why closure was so hard, but the lack of response was a good indication that it was past time to get over it.

Chapter 26

Work continued to be stressful for Kyle during his shifts. Since the deployment for his unit was wrapping up, there was a push conduct tactical events and maneuvers that made an impact in the region that they were deployed to. More raids, more arrests, and more patrols in the local areas near the forward operating base. Each of the events required more intelligence gathering. Therefore, Kyle, CPT Cueva, and the entire section worked relentlessly to provide that intelligence support.

Kyle made it a hobby, or more like an obsession, to look deeper into the multitude of reports that he had access to in order to find clues about the attack that killed Specialist Filner. He made a special folder on his computer to store copies of anything that he found to be related. There were reports about missing workers from the laundry or "washeteria" on the base, various deaths regarding the mishandling of IEDs, and other events around the time of the attack. Kyle started to form a few theories, but he didn't have enough to support them or enough to nominate specific known enemies as future targets for the upcoming raids by his unit or others.

One particular night, Kyle was taking a break from work and went over to the large rock where he and some of the enlisted soldiers used to smoke cigars. Sometimes, some of the other guys would still go there and smoke, but Kyle was unable to return, since it was where Specialist Filner was killed, until then. While no one was there, Kyle sat alone and pondered what happened, his own life, and his future. As his mind metaphorically flipped channels over the multiple subjects, he sat, oblivious to the world around him. He was tired of being in Iraq and wanted to cry, but he couldn't.

In the distance, SGT Bays saw LT Scott and felt compelled to join him but changed his mind. Hanging out at the old spot was too much for him as well after the attack.

After the talk Mr. Scott had with his son during his leave, he had some time to think about a few things. He only wanted the best for his son. Any intrusion from him in his son's life was sincerely just him looking out for him. He fought the urge to email Kyle's commander or to give Kyle too much advice.

Considering all of that, he was torn about what to do when he received a letter from Raven shortly after Kyle had returned to Iraq. At first, he didn't tell his wife about it but sought her advice about the best way to reply.

He called out to her as he sat in his man cave one afternoon. "Clare, could you come down here for a second?" She hesitated a bit when she walked over to him because she was unsure what he needed.

"Baby, I received a letter from Raven and I don't know how to answer it. I actually see that she holds true remorse for her actions, but Kyle doesn't joke around with his feelings like that. You understand what I mean, right?"

Frankly not understanding what her husband meant, Ms. Scott asked for some clarification. "Reggie, what does the letter say?"

Mr. Scott went over parts of the letter with his wife. He was impressed at how mature Raven sounded as she called for a second chance to "show her true feelings". She said in the letter that her "mistake in hurting Kyle" was because she was "foolishly experimenting out of fear of an uncertain future".

Eager to get back to what she was cooking upstairs, and not wanting to get too involved in the situation, she said, "Honey, say what you truly feel, but keep in mind that you were once her age."

Honestly, he already knew what he wanted to say. He wanted to discuss with his wife to get some feeling of justification for what he would eventually write when he responded to her.

Melanie was getting impatient. Ever since her late night rendezvous with Kyle in his trailer, she desperately wanted to finish what they started. The problem was that she didn't see Kyle as much anymore at their secret location or the gym. Their visits grew less frequent, and Kyle was extremely jumpy whenever they did meet. He claimed to be in his office more and working on something important, but she couldn't help but to feel rejected.

Maybe my rank is the problem. I promised him that I wouldn't tell anyone. Maybe he has a woman back home that he is too much of a punk to talk about. Those were some of the thoughts that she had one night while she half-heartedly worked out at the gym. Given the situation of him being unable to publicly show any care about an officer, she had to take his word.

She was more than horny. She gradually acquired feelings Kyle as they conversed on those late nights, and she enjoyed the rush of adrenaline that sneaking around with him gave her. She was going to be returning to the States a little after Kyle was scheduled go back. She was going to try and play it cool, but she had a few tricks up her sleeve to ensure she would not be forgotten. She wanted him to know that she was ready to be more than his occasional groping session with small talk.

At the same time that SSG Sheffield was having those thoughts, Kyle was still in his office stressing about finding intelligence and answers to the questions that he didn't even know. Unbeknownst to her, she was right in part of her thinking – there was a woman in Kyle's thoughts that crept in every so often.

Kyle wasn't the only one sitting in his office late that night. LTC Bloomberg was also sitting behind his closed door with a handwritten note on it that stated "Do Not Disturb – Busy Strategizing". Actually, there no strategizing was going on at the time. He was sipping from a soda bottle that he filled with whiskey. LTC Bloomberg was given a sealed bottle of whiskey by one of the commanders under his purview after a successful raid of a weapons cache.

His subordinate told him, "Sir, it is amazing to see so many bottles of Johnnie Walker in Iraq. What should I do with it?"

He told him, "Son, leave one in my office, keep one for yourself, keep quiet, and report the rest."

The liquor didn't even soothe the battalion commander's angst about the upcoming missions that his unit were about to participate in. His angst was just an excuse for him to drink. The two critical efforts, humorously titled "Operation Fourth and Goal" and "Operation Bottom of the Ninth", could have substantial effects on the war on terror within that region of Iraq. LTC Bloomberg contemplated about how to prepare for his unit's portion of them. He pushed his staff greatly, including CPT Cueva and Kyle, to give constant updates about key elements that fell in their lanes.

Becoming a battalion commander was LTC Bloomberg's ultimate goal when he was a young second lieutenant. Now that he was living his goal, he was being torn apart internally from the stress of commanding during war. He subdued his compassionate nature so he would appear strong and confident to his troops. He was tired of terrorists committing the acts against fellow Soldiers and terrorizing their own communities. He was tired of being around death. Though death was a part of war, each death in 53rd Field Artillery felt extra personal to him. The fact that his participation in the war was coming to an end, gave him some solace. He just had to hold on a little longer and lead his battalion through two more major offensive missions before redeploying back to Fort Stewart and eventually retiring.

He continued to drink, hoping that the liquor would provide some sort of inspiration as much as he hoped it would bring some relaxation. The liquid only made him tipsy, and he regretted ever taking the first sip.

Chapter 27

A week later, Kyle knocked on the Chaplain's door so they could grab some breakfast together before the morning update brief to the commander. He was shocked to see his friend shopping for lingerie for his wife using the FOB's slow internet. The Chaplain noticed the look of surprise on the lieutenant's face and said "I'm just getting ready for the trip back home, K. Scott. I told my wife to be ready for me when I get home, and she told me to get something for her to be ready in." He then roared his typical laugh.

Kyle always thought that even Chaplain Mosley's laugh made him sound like he was preaching a sermon. It wasn't that Kyle was surprised to know of his comrade planning for his reunion with his wife. It was just different to actually see a chaplain shopping for lingerie, whether married or not, simply because he was a man of the cloth. Still seeing the shock on Kyles's face, he stated, "What is the first part of the phrase, 'A Man of God'? That's right . . . a man! K-Man, you know what time it is. Don't even trip, young brother."

They both laughed, and the chaplain closed his computer. They walked over to the dining facility while talking about the types of lingerie that they prefer to see on women. Kyle was better at keeping his shock to himself as his friend was very detailed and seemed to like the kinkier stuff. Kyle on the other hand preferred the lacy, conservative stuff.

Breakfast was uneventful for the most part other than their small talk about random subjects. They were dreading going to the morning meeting. The enthusiasm amongst their unit's staff was obviously dwindling because the focus of going home was so obvious. After getting a cup of coffee to go, they both headed back to the headquarters building.

Kyle took his usual seat behind CPT Cueva in the meeting room minutes before the commander walked in. He gave CPT Cueva a thumbs up signifying that the presentation slides pertaining to the intelligence portion had been updated. He sat in the back row away from the gigantic conference room table that took up most of the space in the wooden and concrete command center. Everyone rose to their feet as LTC Bloomberg boomed into the room to acknowledge his presence. He looked jolly as he spoke to everyone in his usual car salesman voice and told everyone to take their seats.

Usually, the intelligence update followed the agenda slide. CPT Cueva hesitated as the first slide that he was supposed to brief came up. When CPT Cueva spoke, it was obvious to Kyle that he didn't even read the slides beforehand. His boss tap danced through the information and whatever questions that the staff asked him.

Kyle usually sat quiet unless he was asked a specific question, but the overwhelming urge to correct his boss came over him. Maybe it was the fact that he was tired of researching and updating slides just to have his boss stray off of the narrative. Maybe it was just from frustration from dealing with CPT Cueva period.

Either way, Kyle jumped up and said, "Sir, actually, trends over the past week seem to show an increase of activity about five miles east of here. The activities include . . .,"

CPT Cueva attempted to take control back from Kyle and interrupted him. "Yes, there has been activity, but the enemy's focus is more on the . . .,"

Kyle had spent too many hours looking through reports and intelligence databases that week. He felt confident with his assessment and couldn't let CPT Cueva say anything in order to pacify the commander.

Kyle took a step closer to the table as he wrestled the attention back to him by speaking louder. His deeper voice drowned out what CPT Cueva was saying. Chaplain Moseley smiled while most of the other Captains on the staff frowned at Kyle's perceived insubordination. Both of the guys continued talking over one another and were gradually getting louder. After a few minutes, LTC Bloomberg stopped the back and forth bantering between his intelligence officers by saying, "Ok. Enough. You two get some fucking marriage counseling. CPT Cueva, there is clearly an inconsistency in what you two are saying. You come see me around noon and brief me. Ok, let's get on with the meeting."

CPT Cueva was visibly flustered while Kyle sat back down in his chair feeling like a weight had been lifted off of his shoulders. Lieutenants usually cowered in front of that amount of leadership, but Kyle was no stranger to standing up for himself and what was right regardless of who was the recipient.

Later that night, Kyle reluctantly agreed to meet Melanie for some late night conversation. She seemed overly excited during their brief exchange in the gym earlier. He even told her, "Calm down!" in a hushed voice through clenched teeth for fear that people around them would be suspicious. The few people in the gym didn't notice or didn't care enough to think twice about it.

After a lackluster workout, Melanie jogged to her room and headed to the shower trailer near her. She had been thinking about what could be ever since that morning. She was glad that she ran into him on purpose. She was going to be a little bolder since letting Kyle take charge wasn't getting them anywhere. She wanted Kyle emotionally and physically, and that night was going to be the night she had in mind.

She was enveloped by his charm and loved his nerdy side. Their conversations were filled with historical topics and overall positive topics impressed her. She was learning so much from him. His deep, calming voice made her hang on to each word. He was unlike any guy that she had dealt with before. Most of the Army guys that she dated only complained about work or talked about sex. Her daydreams continued to be of her being on his arm at the next military ball or him helping her daughter out with her homework.

Around their typical meeting time and place, Melanie saw Kyle approach cautiously. He ducked behind one of the barriers and came out in the abandoned area where she was waiting. Her heart thumped as she spoke, "Hi."

Kyle caught a whiff of her perfume and leaned in to hug her. "Hey."

She held on to him as he was releasing her from the hug. Kyle squeezed her again and looked into her eyes. He knew that she wanted to kiss him, but he hesitated. Before he could say anything, she forcefully pulled his upper half down to her and went for it.

Kyle couldn't resist and permitted the moment to happen. He placed his weapon on the ground and went in for a second kiss. *Damn, she smells good.* They continued heavy petting for about five minutes. He pinched her nipples as she rubbed his chest. He palmed her ass as she kissed his neck.

Insatiably ready, she felt it was time to make her move. The wetness between her thighs confirmed it. She could hear her own heart beating rapidly as it thumped in her ears. There was not going to be a better time than right then. She pushed him off to grab a towel that she packed in the bag she brought with her. She placed the towel on the ground in front of Kyle and dropped to her knees. She pawed at his shorts with such speed, but with gentleness, when she pulled them down just enough to grab his erect penis.

Before Kyle could utter a word of resistance, he felt the warmness and urgency of her mouth. He tried to resist and wanted to, but couldn't. His knees buckled and he fell back against the wall of the barrier. She scooted forward and kept going. It felt too good to him for her to stop. At the same time, it felt wrong for him to let her continue. He opened his eyes to see her exposed breasts and her shorts pulled down. He almost climaxed right then, but he pushed her head back.

"Stop. Ohhh shit. Please stop."

As he tried to catch his breath, she kept attempting to please him determined to fulfill his desire and hers. "Seriously. I need you to stop," Kyle stated as he literally had a hand on her head to stop her advance. He wanted to continue so badly, but the stories from his dad of peers that got caught up with an enlisted Soldier and thoughts about Raven bounced in his head.

Rejected once again, Melanie jumped up and got dressed. She patted the dust off of her shorts, but she didn't look him in the eye. She was embarrassed and pissed off that she would have to go to bed horny and alone again. She wanted to kiss him, at least, to show that she was genuine in how she felt.

Melanie got the courage to ask a silent Kyle about what he was thinking. Her voice was cracking as she said, "Look, I know that I am a Staff Sergeant and that you are a Lieutenant. I am not out here looking to get you or me in trouble. I really like you…" She paused in order to keep the tears away. "Kyle, Is it someone else? Are you still in love with that other girl? Are you still thinking about her?" She finally looked at him. She could see his mental anguish just as he saw the sincerity in hers.

Kyle sighed and gave a half answer. "I had a girl, but she is my past and no longer my present."

He didn't give an answer to the second part of Melanie's questioning because he still thought about Raven. He hugged her and felt himself rising again. She felt it too. He quickly followed with, "How about we do this? We will both be back home soon. Let's chill and be rational. It is exciting what we are doing here, but we can really enjoy each other without fear of getting caught when we get back."

Melanie started tearing up again and said, "Ok, but you have to kiss me again. Right now."

Without hesitation, Kyle touched her chin and lifted it up until their lips met. The kiss felt freeing to him. The kiss took away all of the stress that he was feeling. There was more truth in that one kiss than he had felt in a while. She felt better and more attracted to him than ever. Afterwards, they stood quietly in the dark, holding each other for a few more minutes before separately sneaking away to head back to their rooms.

Kyle was drained after coming down from the adrenaline of what just happened with Melanie and after a long day. He drank half of a large bottle of tea that he picked up earlier from the nearby shopping center on the base. He reflected on how Melanie's body looked and the sadness in her eyes when he disappointed her again. He later had other random thoughts including CPT Cueva and SPC Filner. He fantasized about his mother's cooking as he drifted off to sleep.

Around 4 in the morning, he suddenly sat up in his bed panting. He had experienced another nightmare. It was similar to the ones he had in the past where his incomplete intelligence assessment caused too many injuries and death. That particular time, the nightmare had more of a twist. In his sleep, he envisioned his mother and Mia sitting next to Raven who was sitting next to Melanie. All were tied up and crying as they begged a terrorist with a bandana on his face to spare them. Kyle called to the man who was aiming an AK-47 toward the ladies. He was ignored at first, but suddenly the mask man pointed the gun toward him and said, "Do you want to save them?" In his dream, he could hear himself saying, "Yes, actually I do." The man pulled his mask down to reveal that he was CPT Cueva. The terrorist, his boss, smiled and replied, "Good", before shooting all four women.

Chapter 28

Jasper was having lunch with Shelia at her place on a Saturday. She ordered a few dishes that she and Jasper had eaten before at a local seafood restaurant to be delivered. All of their clothes were on, and it had been a minute since they had seen each other without any. They were casually eating and talking about various topics. Complaints about work, basketball, parents, and financial investments were some of the subjects that came and went like a person changing channels on a television. Nothing remotely close to sex and their relationship came up, even though it consumed both of their minds.

Jasper trusted that he could be honest with his business-savvy, part-time lover so he waited until there was a break in the conversation and told her about a business idea that he had. He fumbled his words as he tried to convey the desire to take what he learned at work and expand it. He wanted to start small, then expand it to the point where he may be able to do it full time.

Shelia listened to Jasper with curiosity. "So, it seems like you are not being fulfilled at InfoTech Solutions. Maybe you are just bored or maybe you just want something more."

Jasper nodded as he continued to eat.

She continued, "Maybe you see your career like you see women. Bored easily and desirous of something more." Jasper then looked up and saw Shelia weirdly glaring at him.

Jasper suddenly felt that she somehow found a way to make the conversation about her again. He hated when she did that. They could be talk about any random topic, and she would twist it to pertain to her. Jasper was no longer interested in talking about his vision because he didn't want to give her any more ammo to shoot back at him. He smoothly changed the subject. He then felt awkward and started thinking of a reason to leave shortly after they finished eating. He made a mental note to at least pinch her flawless booty a couple of times before departing though.

Meanwhile in Pembrook, Rodney laid in his bed recovering from a bad cold and a terrible dry cough that he had for over a week. He didn't have a performance coming up at Jo Jo's, and the children's choir was going to sing at church the upcoming Sunday. Therefore, he had no scheduled practices for either. He was able to enjoy his couple of days off from his part-time job. He simply needed the rest, and the cold was his body's way of telling him to sit down.

Katrina spent the day studying, and their daughter was at a friend's house for a playdate with her children. Rodney, wanting to take full advantage of the peace and quiet, wanted to make some noise with his wife. As she brought in a hot tottie (which consisted of hot tea, a peppermint, lemon juice, and some whiskey), he prompted her for some sex in his usual passive aggressive way.

"Boy, you need to rest. You over there being mannish instead of getting some sleep and getting over that doggone cold." She dismissed him and headed back to the living room to study. He had been going full throttle lately with his music trying to stay relevant and coming up with new ideas to take the band to the next level. Between that, work, and being a family man, there wasn't much time to rest. Regardless, he wasn't too tired or sick to attempt to get some play from his wife.

"Trina, baby, they say that you have to sweat out a cold after drinking a hot tottie. So…So…I'm just saying that you should help a brother out."

"You are not about to be coughing and sweating on top of me with your sick ass. I got to study anyway."

Ever persistent, Rodney threw back at her, "At least, let me see your ass or half a nipple or something. Shit."

Katrina poked her head in the room and joked at the big man wrapped in blankets. "Rodney, take your ass back to sleep. I might hook you up later." As she walked back to the couch where she had her books open, she heard him still talking.

"I might not want any later!"

Katrina shouted back, "Boy, leave me alone!"

Kyle and CPT Cueva were extremely busy as they gathered as much intelligence as they could to prepare for the upcoming operations. They gave additional updates to the commander outside of the traditional meetings every day. Both were prepping evidence and interviewing detainees when they arrived after the preparatory missions. Both soldiers spent early mornings and late nights in the office.

Despite all of the time they spent together, there was still tension between them. Kyle made it a point to personally inform the commander about any difference in the updates and assessments that were submitted by CPT Cueva instead of blowing up at the staff meetings. Personally, he didn't see anything wrong with his actions, but LTC Bloomberg felt differently. After the third time he made it to his office to give his opinion, Kyle was asked to close the door.

"Listen Lieutenant. I don't know what got you two rubbing each other the wrong way, but I need my intelligence officers to be on one accord. We are days away from "Operation Fourth and Goal". I need my men out there armed with the best Intel that you guys can give them together. Work that shit out."

Kyle felt the urge to say something back to explain, but he knew better and just said, "Yes sir."

Chaplain Mosley told Kyle something similar to what the Commander told him. The problem was obviously CPT Cueva and whatever chip he had on his shoulder. Kyle was the subordinate and was expected to be more humble and compliant. He wanted to let his boss lead, but Kyle was doing the brunt of the work and feeding the results to his irate superior. He was tired of getting yelled at for no reason and tired of CPT Cueva giving opinionated updates that really weren't supported by facts or the intelligence that was gathered.

On top of that, Kyle learned that he hadn't been recommended for an end-of-deployment award. It was typical for Soldiers, especially the staff, to be acknowledged for their tireless work while being deployed. Sergeant First Class Carson, who was a black woman, pulled him aside and told him how the three black officers on the staff were either not recommended for an award or were nominated for a lesser award than the others. This included him and Chaplain Mosley.

Needless to say, Kyle carried that irritation with him as he dealt with CPT Cueva because he was the one who recommended and filled out the required paperwork for the award. Of course, Kyle wanted the same award that the other staff members would receive. At the same time, he was cautious not to stir up trouble after his last talk with LTC Bloomberg. He wasn't going to let the issue go away and decided to bring it up at the right time. Until then, he had a job to do. Chaplain Mosley told Kyle that he would look into it. Chaplain Mosley understood that his own job was thankless and found reward in being a counselor and pastor to as many Soldiers that would listen. He didn't want the young lieutenant to become jaded so early in his career, especially with his eagerness to learn and proven tenacity during combat.

Chapter 29

The dream started off differently from most of the ones in the past. There was a large meeting with the staff, but Kyle was at the head of the table instead of the commander. Everyone was yelling about various things to Kyle as he just sat there unable to speak or move. He wanted to speak and wanted to tell everyone to "Shut up!", but he couldn't. All he could do was sit there since he didn't have a mouth in the dream.

The staff berated him with ideas of what should be done in many unrelated arguments. One argued that chocolate chip cookies were better than oatmeal cookies. Another argued that Second Lieutenants shouldn't be in the Army. Chaplain Mosley was at the opposite end of the table telling Kyle to pray more. Captain Cueva was in the dream as well and was yelling that the latest intelligence report showed a squad of terrorist Beagles were staging an attack near the city of Puppy Chow in three days.

Hearing CPT Cueva make his statement caused Kyle to say out loud, "That's silly." Gasps and boos ensued but then the staff stopped talking simultaneously and looked at Kyle. He was then dragged out of the headquarters and thrown into a prison cell where Specialist Filner and his father were sitting on the same rock where he used to smoke cigars. No one was smoking though.

As Kyle walked up to them, he could overhear his father tell Specialist Filner, "He didn't know better. He is only a lieutenant."

Filner kept asking "Why? Why?"

Each time his father would say something like, "It is not his fault that he didn't do enough. He didn't listen to me, and I told Fuzz to listen to me."

Kyle stood there unable to talk again. He could see the words forming in his mind, but his lips had disappeared.

Kyle woke up from his nightmare confused. He remembered all of the details and felt panicky. He wondered if there was a message in what he had just dreamt, but the awkwardness of the details dominated the meanings of the different pieces. Kyle sleepily whispered, "Puppy Chow?" before laying back down to go back to sleep.

"Operation Fourth and Goal" was days away from execution. The 53rd Field Artillery, Kyle's unit, had a key objective in the operation, which was to set up checkpoints in a specific area of one of the nearby cities known to be a hotbed of terrorist activity. Accurate intelligence was critical for discerning what routes needed to be clear and which areas were prime to set up checkpoints.

During the previous weeks, another unit, the 26th Infantry Battalion, had arrived to conduct a left seat, right seat ride with the 53rd Field Artillery. A "left seat, right seat ride" is the term used when the exiting unit hands over the mission by conducting operations with the entering unit shadowing them and eventually taking over. 53rd Field Artillery would lead their portion of the planned operation. As planned, the 26th Infantry Battalion would be more in charge of the final operation before 53rd's redeployment.

The frequency of meetings increased among the staff, along with the updates to the commander. The maintenance personnel worked extra hours to get all of the vehicles combat ready. Burnout was evident in the faces of the staff, but everyone kept pushing. There were also visits from staff officers from the upper military echelons which kept everyone on their toes.

At the same time, non-critical parts of the unit were preparing for redeployment back to the United States. Inventories and the packing of excess equipment had begun. The lines at the little post office on the FOB seemed to get longer everyday as Soldiers sent home extra items and gifts that they bought for themselves and loved ones. The gym seemed to be a little more packed in the mornings as people attempted to tighten up their bodies before going back home.

Kyle carried the thoughts of his most recent nightmare with him as he worked leading up to the upcoming battle. He also carried the optimism about going home soon. LTC Bloomberg and CPT Mosley suggested that he made peace with CPT Cueva, so Kyle invited his boss to have dinner with him. The disgruntled intelligence officer quickly turned the invitation down and asked him for a status update instead. Frustrated, Kyle exhaled and said, "Sir, I will get that to you shortly." He returned to his desk thinking, *Fuck it. I tried.*

Two days later, the primary staff of 53rd Field Artillery were gathering for their usual morning huddle with the commander. Everyone looked more tired than usual. Most of them were silent and held back on the occasional good morning greetings. Everyone was waiting to go through this daily formality so they could get on with the rest of the day.

Chaplain Mosley, who was older than most of the other Captains in the room, walked in cheerfully, shaking hands, and making idle chit chat. CPT Cueva yawned when he walked in and took his seat. He didn't speak to anyone while he drank a cup of coffee. Kyle walked in shortly after and took his usual seat behind his boss.

Around 8:15, the commander rushed into the conference room and walked toward his seat. Everyone jumped up and stood at attention. As the commander took his seat, everyone followed suit and sat down.

"I'm sorry that I am late, but I just got off of the phone with Lieutenant General Thomas who is sitting in Kuwait right now. He told me to tell you guys 'great job' and to keep pushing until this thing is done. HOOAH!!!"

Most of the officers and noncommissioned officers replied back less enthusiastically, "HOOAH!"

"Ok, let's get started. Weather." LTC Bloomberg looked in Kyle's direction who had been unwillingly reduced to only telling the weather forecast and other little tidbits of information in the morning meetings. CPT Cueva, in a show of dominance, stopped allowing Kyle to brief the actions and trends of the enemy forces.

Kyle began, "Good morning, sir. The screen shows the forecasted weather for the next few days. "Today, we are expecting typical weather with a possible gusty winds later this afternoon." Kyle continued his report and then sat down. He was thanked by the commander as the meeting continued with CPT Cueva.

CPT Cueva took his notes that were mostly prepared by Kyle, and started to read them. He wasn't energetic at all as he sighed between reading the notes that corresponded with the presentation slides that were projected on the large screen. He was in the middle of reading his notes when Kyle kept noisily shifting in his chair.

CPT Cueva looked back to Kyle with a perturbed glance and continued on, "You see, sir. The tendency of that particular cell is to use paid off non-military civilians to place the IEDs and act as lookouts for friendly forces. Ummm . . . also, we noticed that they conduct what I would call intimidation patrols to influence cooperation with their cause."

"No disrespect, sir, but you are wrong with this one. My analysis shows different. What you said isn't totally true. You have to trust me on this one, but you usually don't."

Silence and astonishment enveloped the room as the last part of Kyle's statement was a definite jab at his supervisor. Without caring, Kyle continued as CPT Cueva was noticeably agitated and turning red as he glared at him.

"Sir, it seems like some of the civilians in that area don't really support the cause, but they are rather unsympathetic to either cause – ours and those of the enemy. The assessment from the Division Headquarters expounds rather extensively regarding that particular neighborhood. They actually pay the terrorist cell to keep the IEDs *out* of their area. They are not particularly anti-American and . . .,"

CPT Cueva had heard enough and was furious that he was being undermined by Kyle in front of the staff again. In an attempt to regain control, he sat up in his chair and spoke up against Kyle. "Ok, LT Scott. The reports from Division Headquarters mentions that as a theory, but there has been little effort to confirm that. Therefore, it is imperative that we take no chances and increase patrols in that neighborhood."

Kyle jumped in, "Sir, if you look at the slide that depicts the known IED emplacements over the last five months, you will see that no others appeared in that neighborhood since March. Yet, you didn't see that IED emplacements grew significantly in the southern border where there are less affluent shop owners and civilians."

There was an awkward pause. CPT Cueva tapped his foot and continued to glare at Kyle. He knew that there was some merit to what Kyle had just said, but the manner in which it came out, stirred up his previous animosity toward him again.

CPT Godfrey, the logistics officer, broke the silence when he said, "Wow."

That only infuriated CPT Cueva more, and he started barking again, "Kyle, get out of here and stand by my desk until this meeting is over!"

Kyle, on the other hand, defiantly maintained his posture and remained in his chair.

LTC Bloomberg looked at the commander of the 26th Infantry who sat next to him and smiled out of embarrassment. He had warned his intelligence officers about showing their failure to cooperate, and he felt that he had to do some barking himself.

"Damn it. I told you two. I need some goddamn Intel, and I get this inconsistent data along with a side of constant bickering. Intel drives the operation, and damn it, I need this operation to go off smoothly. The last thing I need is a goddamn pissing contest fucking that up. Do you hear me?" Kyle and CPT Cueva both sat in silence. "I said, do you fucking hear me?!"

Both men said simultaneously, "Yes sir."

The commander stood up and kept his words spewing about the debacle that he just witnessed.

"Damnit, LT get out of this meeting and wait at your desk until I come get you. CPT Cueva, I would tell you the same, but you two might end up fighting and tear this TOC down. You get out of here too, and standby right outside to get some goddamn air to cool off. Fuck! What is this people?"

The two intelligence officers didn't look at each other as they left the meeting. Kyle allowed CPT Cueva to walk out first to avoid conflict.

LTC Bloomberg, who was now red in the face himself, sat back down and took a deep breath. The rest of the staff sat in silence and in shock after what had happened.

"Chaplain, later, I need you to talk to these two officers and give them some anger management solutions or some shit to resolve this shit. If you are too close to LT Scott, find another chaplain to talk to him. Fuck!"

Chaplain Mosley nodded. After another deep breath, he heatedly said, "Let's continue the fucking meeting . . . unless anyone else wants to get kicked out. What's next?"

Kyle went to his desk and tried to send his father an email on the slow tactical internet. Part of him felt vindicated for standing up to his boss, but he was more worried about how bad LTC Bloomberg would chastise him with it being so close to redeployment. He couldn't allow the Soldiers in his unit to act upon faulty and offhanded assessments, and he had no regrets about what happened. He was gearing up to fight his stance to the commander as well.

After the meeting, LTC Bloomberg walked out of the meeting still pissed off about the earlier flare up between his two intelligence officers. He stomped out after the meeting to find Lieutenant Scott. He stopped in the hallway and yelled to Chaplain Mosley, "Chap, go talk to Cueva and calm his ass down. I see him outside fucking pacing."

Chaplain Mosley hopped up and walked toward the entrance as ordered. The commander started his energetic gait until he made it to his intelligence office.

All of the Soldiers inside of the office snapped to attention when the commander walked in the room. He calmly and firmly said, "I need all of you to give me and the lieutenant a few minutes to talk. Now!"

Without hesitation, everyone walked out but was wondering what Kyle did to get that type of attention. Once they all left, LTC Bloomberg went in on him.

"L-T, what the hell was that? Cueva is not the friendliest guy. Hell, I couldn't see myself having a scotch with the lad, but fuck L-T!"

Kyle's earlier arrogance and desire to further defend himself crumbled. He tried to mumble a response, but he was met with more loud words from the sweating and aggravated commander.

"You know your father was the same fucking way. Boastful, had a way with words, and pissed everybody off." He laughed full-heartedly. "I was only a Captain when he was my current rank and a commander. I wasn't on his staff, but he was known by reputation amongst the officers at Fort Bragg. He

challenged everybody. It was just a good thing that he was right
most of the time. He was impressive, but he came off as cocky
and overbearing to some. He is a proud man. You remind me of
what I remember about him back them.

They talked for a few more minutes with LTC Bloomberg
half scolding him and half giving him advice. He ended with,
"LT Scott, you need to control yourself. There is a better way to
get your point across. Give me a report about what you were
talking about earlier, and we won't tell CPT Cueva. Now, get to
work. HOOAH!"

Kyle smiled, but he was bracing himself for whenever
CPT Cueva walked back into the office.

Chaplain Mosley and Kyle's supervisor were inside of his
trailer continuing their conversation. Since CPT Cueva was
getting loud right outside of the operations center about some
rather personal things, the chaplain suggested that they finish
their talk elsewhere. Chaplain Mosley listened to what seemed
to be a man going through a lot of turmoil from his life back in
the states who finally got a chance to get some of it off of his
chest.

CPT Cueva was dealing with a sick father at home. Also,
he was under constant pressure to support his family financially.

Being one of the few siblings that went to and graduated from college, his family always leaned on him for support.

"You see, I hate the Army. I wanted to get out before this job, but my family called me a failure. I go to my room every day and think about that. I'm just trying to do my job, make it back, and find something to do on the outside. I'm tired of this shit. Forget my family. I want to move to California or Florida and start over."

Chaplain Mosley patiently listened and inserted advice and scriptures when it was appropriate. He hoped that Kyle's boss only needed to vent and would stop taking his internal struggles out on his subordinates. After he reached a point of calm, the two Captains talked about coping techniques. CPT Cueva thanked his fellow staff member for the talk, but he still felt some animosity toward Kyle. How he defied him wouldn't go unnoticed, but Chaplain Mosley was right when he told him that he had "a job to do that is bigger than all of this."

That evening, left the TOC and headed to the gym where he saw Melanie. They regarded each other nonverbally. Kyle wanted to hang out with her again, but didn't want her to think that they were back on again. He wasn't sure if she was just there to really work out or as an attempt to hang out again. He stayed strong against the wave of lust that faced him and completed a lackluster workout

On the way back to his trailer, Kyle revisited the rock where he and some of the Soldiers used to hang out. He brought a cigar with him, but he couldn't bring himself to smoke it. He just sat on the rock and reflected on the day's events as well as his deployment over all. He was so ready to go home especially after the blow up during the morning meeting and the impending awkwardness once CPT Cueva returned to the office.

Sergeant Bays occasionally came to the rock to smoke a cigarette partially out of habit and partially to memorialize his former roommate. He saluted Kyle and commenced with small talk. Kyle didn't mind his company, but preferred the solitude.

Bays said, "Sir, we should have a little memorial for our fallen comrade. Right here. Whatcha think?"

"That would be pretty cool. I think we should. When?" Kyle thought that it was a good idea and was ready to attend the ceremony as long as his work allowed it. The next statement that he heard shocked him though.

"Sir, could you say a few words when we do it? You have a nice speaking voice. You should narrate movies or read books or some shit like that when you get out of the Army."

Kyle laughed for a couple of minutes and then said, "Yeah man. I don't mind at all."

The two of them talked for a few moments to discuss the details and possible times to conduct the ceremony.

Chapter 30

The day before "Operation Fourth and Goal" was sort of like the calm before the storm. The weeks prior to the operation were filled with briefings and planning meetings about the operation or redeployment. All of the inspections and battle preparations were completed. All patrols were cancelled and picked up by other units. Commanders reduced their manning to a minimum in order to give time for everyone to prepare mentally and physically, for the event to come.

Chaplain Mosley was very busy leading up the eve of the operation with events at the chapel and individual counseling sessions. Kyle didn't hang with him much during that time. He spent his time listening to music in is room or was in the gym getting his body extra-toned for the return home. Most Soldiers in the 53rd Field Artillery enjoyed the extra time off and spent their time doing various things. The internet café and phone trailers stayed full and had long lines. The local shopping area and bazaar was busier than usual as people bought gifts for themselves and others.

The dining facility usually served steak and seafood or "surf and turf" on Fridays, but it was being served on that particular Wednesday. Many that partook of the more exquisite cuisine saw the move as a morale booster and a celebration of the last battles before the end of their deployment tour. Some conspired that the true reason for the steak, lobster tails, and extra desserts was for a more morbid reason. Unfortunately, it could have been the last meal for some that were there.

LTC Bloomberg was visibly the most stressed Soldier in the dining facility that night. He slowly ate two steaks, a piece of cake and two cookies. Afterwards, he walked around and shook hands, laughed at jokes, and stopped by table to table amongst his Soldiers and some Soldiers from the other units. Though his face was all grins, his eyes told his truth. He was tired and nervous about the battle that was mere hours away from commencing.

Around midnight, a large number of Soldiers from the 53rd Field Artillery and other units donned their tactical vests, reported to their squads, and made final preparations before proceeding to their respective locations to initiate "Operation Fourth and Goal". Several of the staff members arrived, still a bit sleepy, to the TOC as key leaders were mandated to perform key tasks within their functions if needed. Kyle and some of the secondary staff showed up to the TOC more out of curiosity than necessity. They wanted to be a part of the action even if only to listen to the mission execution over the radios or watch moving icons on the various screens.

There was a kind of nervous excitement going on amongst the staff that was comparable to spectators just before an afterschool tussle. Everyone was trying to get a metaphorical front row view of the fight, but no one wanted anyone to get hurt. All of those extra hours and meetings culminated to that moment. It was the last major battle for the 53rd Field Artillery. Radios squelched with updates and the progress reports were typed on multiple computers.

As the last vehicles rolled out of the FOB to move in to their positions, Kyle grabbed a cup of coffee and stayed in the shadows to listen. The commander used most of Kyle's intelligence assessment that he gave him behind closed doors. CPT Cueva wasn't too thrilled with the fact that his assessment wasn't used, but he couldn't refute the validity of what was put together.

Aqeel Abboud was awakened from his sleep by one of his fellow brethren. He excitedly whispered to Aqeel in Arabic, "We need to get out of here. The Americans are setting up down the street. We need to get out of here." Aqeel rubbed his eyes and saw that others were packing up weapons and trying to make their place less suspicious in case it was raided. The same comrade kicked at his feet and said again, "We need to get out of here." The five men in the semi-abandoned building grabbed what they could and prepared to make a run for safer locations away from where the "Infidel" Americans were suspected to be.

Aqeel could hear the military vehicles not too far away from their location. One of the five men at the location ran back to the building frantically and told the others that some of the dwellings not too far from them was being checked for weapons. Aqueel's heart was racing as he felt fear of being caught or worse. He didn't want to be there, but he chose to volunteer to occupy the location as he sought favor and wanted to impress his superiors. Favor meant more responsibility, which meant more money and power.

The guy deemed to be in charge of the huddled the small group for some quick instructions on hiding the IEDs and weapons that they had on them. Once he finished speaking it was as if every man was for himself. The group of terrorists scattered to find hiding places or tried to leave so they could get back to their homes. Aqeel, who wasn't too familiar with that particular section of town, blindly followed behind one of the others. Wherever that guy went, Aqeel stayed close to him in hopes that they would both escape the intruding forces that awoke the citizens and rudely searched their homes in the night and darkness.

The Abna Aleadala had a reputation of never getting caught and were highly regarded amongst the local Al Qaeda. That was about to change. The sounds of tactical vehicles and Soldiers seemed to be around every major road or alley blocking an easy escape. Aqeel and the man he was following eventually found themselves trapped at a dead end. They hid on opposite sides of the back street hoping to remain overlooked in the darkness. At that moment, Aqeel wished that he had never been seduced by greed and joined the Sons of Justice. He wish that he was at home with his brother.

As the Americans who were patrolling that sector got closer, Aqeel's comrade started to pace anxiously. The commotion attracted the attention of one of the Soldiers from the 26th Infantry Battalion. In a mixture of adrenaline and eagerness to use his training, the 1st Lieutenant Jeffrey Bergeson ordered a squad patrol to check it out as he and a few others blocked off the entrance. It was a decision that he would later regret because one of the two Abna Aleadala members was eager to die for the cause that he vehemently pledged allegiance to.

Three Soldiers with M16 rifles outfitted with bright flashlight attachments walked down the alley in a slow, deliberate formation. Once they got toward the end, they found a man cowering in one of the corners with his hands up. He was crying and mumbling incomprehensively. Before the squad leader could call it in to the Lieutenant, a flurry of shots rang out from an AK-47 hitting the rear man of the three soldiers who were ordered to investigate.

The other two spun around to see the man that Aqeel had followed aiming at them, and they returned fired and shot him multiple times eliminated any further threat. Once the shooting stopped, Aqeel remained cowering in the corner in a total state of surrender. Sergeant Christopher Snell laid on the ground with multiple gunshots, fighting for his life. His legs took heavy fire and one bullet unfortunately struck under his left armpit and pierced his left lung.

Around two in the morning, some of the staff had started to retreat to their offices or trailers as the excitement of the battle started to wane. Kyle rarely ate "midnight chow", which was the limited selection of food served at the dining facility between dinner and breakfast for Soldiers who returned from various patrols or guard duty. As he opened his Styrofoam container to grab another slice of cold pizza, traffic on one of the monitored radio channels picked up some frantic chatter.

Everyone who was still around perked up with anticipation that a firefight or something else exciting had happened. What came through over the radio was a fast-talking LT Bergeson calling in a situation report about what had just transpired. Medical support was being called to be prepared to accept an incoming Soldier shot while on patrol. Jaws dropped and shoulders slumped as more details came. Reports were passed to the upper echelons, and the staff in the operations center scrambled to react as needed.

Reports and inquiries for the injured Soldier influenced the commanders on the ground to begin more aggressive reconnaissance. Kyle overheard one of the commanders calling in over the radio requesting to pursue an alleged terrorist known to be in the area of operations. An Iraqi national that was stopped at one of the checkpoints offered information about a group of men that occasional took over his place when they were conducting business in that vicinity. That, and information obtained from the detainee found crying at the scene where Sergeant Snell was shot, gave Soldiers in the area more focus.

53rd Field Artillery and other units involved in "Operation Fourth and Goal" was originally conducting a show of force mission with multiple targeted locations. Knocking on doors and randomly searching homes would do two things. It would show that the new forces where coming to town and weren't punks, and the actual search for known targets may piss off enough of the locals so they would possibly point out the terrorists. Word would spread quickly, even at the early morning hour that a Soldier was injured and it wasn't appreciated by the U.S. Forces.

Around five in the morning, the mission was coming to a close. Kyle and CPT Cueva both had to do some precursory interviewing of five detainees who were captured during the operation. The translators helped with the interview just prior to Kyle and CPT Cueva taking the detainees to a permanent facility. There was no exhibition of loyalty in the face of those caught; only self-preservation. During the interview, one particular detainee, Aqeel, told multiple stories with the hope of being set free. He figured that he would be killed if he were sent to prison or seen being captured by the U.S. Army.

One particular story gave Kyle the closure that he needed. He listened from over CPT Cueva's shoulder as Aqeel talked about his first mission. It was to sneak in a GPS device and give occasional coordinates to his terrorist cell. As Kyle listened, he figured out that the man who was responsible for Specialist Filner's death, sat inches away from him in handcuffs. Finally, he had made eye contact with the man responsible for many of his late nights of regret and extra hours spent in the office. He clenched his fists and swallowed a few times since his throat suddenly felt dry.

Through the translator, Kyle said to Aqeel, "He was a good man. You know that? Huh?" He looked angrily at the man for a few more minutes trying to maintain his composure. The prisoner was afraid and looking bewildered as he saw Kyle's fists starting to shake.

CPT Cueva was on the other side of the temporary detainee area finishing up a couple of reports when he suddenly heard a lot of commotion and screaming. He spun around to see Kyle shaking and yanking the shirt of Aqeel as he yelled, "It's your fault! It's your fault!" One of the interpreters and CPT Cueva pulled Kyle off of the prisoner and toward the door.

"What the hell is wrong with you? You can't do this shit, Lieutenant Scott!!" CPT Cueva saw his subordinate as somewhat of a hothead, but he was not expecting what just occurred. Kyle's hands were still shaking. CPT Cueva saw that and continued, "What do you mean 'your fault'?"

Kyle swallowed and said, "He is the missing laundry worker in the reports. He had something to do with the mortar attack that went down while I was on leave." His boss looked at Aqeel, then back at Kyle, and replied, "Oh."

CPT Cueva took the opportunity to make a peace offering to Kyle. He waited until Kyle had calmed down some before walking over to him and whispering to him, "Ok. This is what you do. When the interpreters and I walk outside in a few minutes, you go get one more shove in." Kyle smiled in response. CPT Cueva reiterated, "Look, get one more shove in, but no punching or anything. Then go."

Kyle nodded in silent agreement then waited. As promised, CPT Cueva and the interpreter stepped outside the tent to talk. Kyle glared at Aqeel as he advanced and placed his pointer finger to his lips to tell Aqeel to stay silent. He could see the captured terrorist's fear and submission in his eyes. He enjoyed it way too much as he mushed Aqeel's head so hard that he fell out of the chair that he was sitting in. Kyle walked away both very tired and very satisfied.

Chapter 31

Jasper stirred a little bit after his phone buzzed to notify him that he had a new text message. He looked at his alarm clock and saw that it was too early for someone to be texting him and ignored it. Then he looked at the woman who was lying next to him snoring slightly. A mixed feeling of achievement and regret came over him at the same time. It was more like the pride from the previous night's conquest would be surpassed by worry about the aftermath that would ensue when she awoke.

All three of the "Men of 1302" and some of their former classmates amusingly called her "Pretty Titty Vivian". Jasper swore that he wouldn't ever touch her again, but she happened to call at the right time when Jasper was feeling up for the challenge. The awkwardness of sleeping with his former fiancé's friend and sorority sister, was greatly overshadowed by her tendency to be clingy and aggressive when desirous for sex.

Other than seeing her beautifully flawless areolas, the few that knew Vivian sexually, understood that she wasn't an easy bull to ride, per se. Her height along with her firm, but feminine stature, made lesser men think twice before "climbing that mountain", as Jasper's dad would say. Jasper made sure to take a nap and stretch before she arrived to his apartment in Cordova. Kyle called her a "PT test", while Rodney called her a "donk and drama package". Regardless of what she was called, Jasper came out on top in the aerobic session of simply fucking with no passion, but he knew that he would spend a large part of that Saturday napping after she left.

Vivian laid there still asleep in Jasper's bed as his phone buzzed again. Choosing to not ignore it this time just in case it was someone of importance, he rolled over to grab it. It was Rodney. He texted Jasper to see if he was up. He wanted Jasper to listen to the bassline of an Outkast song that he was working on at the moment.

Rodney was known to sleep very little once an idea to create new music popped into his head. No different from when they were roommates, he beckoned Jasper for an opinion.

Once Jasper replied, Rodney quickly texted:

`Whatcha up to? Hit me up.`

`        Dude, why?  It's like 9 a.m. On a Saturday.`

Wake your ass up.   I want you to listen to this.   This Outkast song is tight bruh, but it's missing something.

Jasper really wanted to just go back to sleep, so he tried to get his friend to text him later.

Mane, I will hit you up later.

Rodney, ever the persistent bully, kept pushing.

Bruh I just need a few minutes

Then you can take your punk ass back to sleep.

I'm next to Pretty Titty. She's sleep.

Oh shit!   Hit me up later.

Glad to end the conversation, Jasper placed his phone back down by his alarm clock and looked to see if Vivian was still asleep. He got back under the covers and laid on his side of his bed away from the nude woman who shared it with him. Minutes later, as he was dozing back off, he felt her hand moving toward him. Not ready for a round two, he played like he was asleep until she calmed down.

"Operation Fourth and Goal" was an overall success considering the prescribed goals for each of the military units involved. There was a general feeling amongst the Soldiers on Forward Operating Base Justice similar to that of coming down off of an adrenaline high from a championship football game. Some of the amped up Soldiers were fatigued and distressed by what they just went through. It was time to recover and get ready for the next mission. "Operation Bottom of the Ninth" was less than a week away, and it was estimated to be just as hectic as the previous one.

In between that time, Sergeant Bays and Kyle got a second to host a small memorial for Specialist Filner. CPT Cueva didn't object to Kyle leaving work for a while to do so. Around three in the afternoon on the following Wednesday, several Soldiers gathered. They included Filner's former squad mates, most of the crew that used to smoke at the rock, and curious onlookers.

Kyle, eager to get it over with before he became too emotional, rushed the beginning of his speech. Not much of a public speaker, he cleared his throat several times as he tried to stay on script with the words he jotted down in his green notebook. He thanked everyone for coming out. He acknowledged special guests and high ranking officials. He wanted not to cry.

While he spoke, he calmed down and no longer needed his notes. His heartfelt words started to flow with ease as he looked past his guilt and focused on honoring a man close to his age that made the ultimate sacrifice. He wasn't as verbose as Chaplain Moseley, but he tried to think of what else he would say during a memorial.

Kyle saw his buddy in the audience and said, "A good friend always told me, and I can't remember the verse exactly, but 'where two or three are gathered in His name, that He is among them'. God is among us right now, and Filner is standing next to him doing that annoying laugh that he used to do." He looked at a tearful SGT Bays and said, "He would be fussing with Bays over there about putting his lighter in his pocket if he was here, or he would be talking about comic books. The whole time he would be smiling and laughing. Even if his laugh *was* weird." Some of the others chuckled. "Kyle finished up with, "We will miss you, Filner. Please look down on us as we prepare to go into our last battle before we redeploy."

SGT Bays dried his tears and walked over to the Humvee. SGT Jefferson helped him pull a heavy object out of the back. They pulled a large painted rock and placed it near the much larger rock where they had congregated. Bay smiled as it was his turn to speak and said, "We decided to paint this to remember our battle buddy. He liked Wolverine and the X-Men." He paused to stop himself from crying again. "He liked Wolverine so we painted a small one on here with his name, date of birth and date of his death. We won't forget you."

Everyone clapped as a couple of guys pushed it closer to the larger rock. After the applause, SGT Bays looked at Kyle and said, "Sir, I have been holding these for a while. These are two cigars that belonged to Specialist Filner. His brother sent one for him and one for you. Filner talked about you all of the time, and his brother wanted to show his appreciation for being his friend."

Kyle began tearing up as the expensive cigar was handed to him. SGT Bays continued, "Since he is not here to enjoy it, I say you and I enjoy them for him." Those amassed in support clapped and hooted as the two lit their cigars and puffed a few times.

The crowd slowly dispersed after that. Chaplain Mosley came up to Kyle and said, "That was good, my brother. I know that Filner was looking down from above and is smiling right now. Good job, K. Scott."

Minutes later, CPT Cueva, walked over to Kyle, shook his hand, and to his surprise said, "That was pretty cool of you."

SSG Sheffield and Kyle made eye contact briefly and Kyle nodded.

The premium cigar that Kyle was smoking, burned nice and slow. Some of the old smoking crew and some new faces lingered and lit up cigars and cigarettes in remembrance of the fallen comrade. After the smoking was over, Kyle headed back to his trailer to take a shower and a nap. He felt a sense of relief as some of the guilt had gone away. He was finally able to get some closure from the tragic situation.

The handover between 53rd Field Artillery and the 26th Infantry Battalion was going well. Counterparts from the two staffs were glued at the hip. Kyle and his counterpart got along fine and discussed similar issues they had with their bosses. More meetings occurred during their busy time to discuss the handover and preparation for the final operation. For one unit, the long hours of hot, desert days would be coming to an end. For the new unit, theirs were just beginning.

At the beginning of a staff meeting between "Operation Fourth and Goal" and "Operation Bottom of the Ninth", LTC Bloomberg sat next to the somber-looking commander of 26th Infantry Battalion. For the incoming commander, he had just experienced the first death of a Soldier under his command. Sergeant Christopher Snell succumbed to his wounds the day prior. It was a feeling that LTC Bloomberg knew too well, unfortunately. The look on the 26th Infantry Battalion Commander's face dampened the mood of the outgoing staff who was excited with almost being done. It was evident that he was human and felt the same conflicting emotions that many other commanders had. At times, a Soldier's death questions a leader's human desire to mourn while having to stay strong for those still alive.

Sensing the need to give one of his motivational pep talks, LTC Bloomberg began the meeting before turning it over to his counterpart. "Ok folks. This has been a long and painful game that we played here. We have received some strikes just as we have received some outs, but we also threw some strikes and tagged a few of these terrorist motherfuckers out. Hell, we even popped a couple of doubles and bunted a few times." The mood of everyone lightened a little bit. "We are in the ninth inning, and it is time for a homerun to take us on home! We have a little more to do, and then we tell this goddamn country 'goodbye and good riddance'!"

Most of the staff hooted and hollered for a couple of minutes including the commander of 26th Infantry. LTC Bloomberg continued, "We are almost home people, and why did – why did that young Sergeant have to die?" Tears filled the eyes of the hard-hitting leader, but he kept talking. "Think about going . . . getting past this last hurdle until we go home. Whatever is your soul's motivation . . . let that drive you in these last days." After taking a few seconds to console himself, he took a very deep breath and sat down. He continued, "I need you all to be 120% until we get home. The changing of the guard happens after this next mission, and 53rd, we are going to give them everything that they need to be successful. HOOAH!!"

Everyone replied with a very enthusiastic "HOOAH", and the rest of the meeting went on successfully. Everyone seemed more energized after receiving the much needed pep talk.

Later that night, Kyle returned to his trailer and grabbed his MP3 player. The battery was low, but he turned it on anyway. He searched through the songs until he found the track that he was looking for. He configured it to play on repeat and plugged it into a set of small speakers that he acquired at the FOB's Post Exchange store. As the smooth instrumentation of *Zoom* by the Commodores began, Kyle flopped on the bed and listened to it until the battery died.

Zoom always had a meditative effect on Kyle. He reflected on what went on during the war. He thought about what his commander said and pondered his emotional words. He thought about what his "soul's motivation" was. Images of his family and friends popped into his head. He remembered what happened on September 11th. He contemplated about his desire to succeed, and how his career was just beginning. He dozed off while fantasizing about what awaited him when he got home.

Even later that night, LTC Bloomberg sat alone in his office. He took in the dry dusty air and took a swig of whiskey placed in a Coke bottle. He picked up the receiver of the tactical phone in his office and dialed the appropriate codes on his privileged extension to connect to the United States. After a couple of transfers, his wife picked up the phone.

After greetings and small talk, he calmly said, "Honey, it's time for me to retire when I get back. I've had a good run." His wife knew how bad he wanted to fight for a chance to be promoted to Colonel. The dejectedness in his voice told her that he was ready to retire despite how promising being Colonel was. He had had enough.

In an attempt to lighten the mood, she joked and said, "Well, sugar, I better enjoy my alone time now before you stay at home bothering me and being bored all day."

Mrs. Bloomberg had met her husband when he was a young Captain serving at Fort Bragg. Their love never wavered despite the years of assignments and deployments that often kept them apart. A lot of spouses were not as supportive. LTC Bloomberg recognized that he had a strong woman who had his back through it all.

"This is my last week in my office, so I will call when I can. Honey, it's time to do something that you want to do. You have been there for me."

"I would do it all again. You be safe. I love you."

Chapter 32

"Operation Bottom of the Ninth" was successful. The intent of the higher echelons of command were met. The commander of the 26th Infantry Battalion got an opportunity to lead his Soldiers into actual battle, thus giving him the confidence back that was previously shaken. It also affirmed to the Iraqi citizens who lived outside of FOB Justice that patrolling the area was not going to slack up with a new unit. It was the conclusion of tactical operations for 53rd Field Artillery. Most importantly, there were no more fatalities.

The final days of the deployment for the 53rd Artillery and other Soldiers, was filled with minimal meetings, personal and tactical equipment being packed, and other activities to prepare for the trip back to Fort Stewart, Georgia. Soldiers of all ranks had a chance to really enjoy the MWR facilities that offered movies, video games, and additional snacks. It had started to feel to Kyle and the others that going home was an actuality.

To commemorate the passing of the baton between the two units, there was a ceremony in front of the headquarters building. LTC Bloomberg had the boom back in his voice and erectness of posture that he had at the beginning of the deployment. He revved up everyone with a speech that thanked them for their part whether big or small, in a successful deployment and remembered all of those "who made the ultimate sacrifice". It was a joyous occasion that ended with the cutting of a large cake inside of the headquarters that stated, "53rd – Job Well Done!!!"

Days later, Kyle stood amongst the first heading back to Fort Stewart from his unit. Since he was junior to CPT Cueva, he was tasked to go back to hold things down for his section until CPT Cueva returned on a later flight. He had stayed up most of the night, mainly out of excitement and anticipation. He called his parents, Mia, and his other friends that he would see soon.

There was a small formation giving last minute details and administrative notes. A small detail was requested to load duffle bags and small equipment on a couple of the trucks nearby. Kyle raised his hand to volunteer, which got him some weird looks. No one expected an officer to jump up to join a detail to do manual labor. He really didn't care or see what the big deal was. He felt he wasn't above anyone in that regard, although his rank was higher than many of the people standing there.

After the duffle bags were packed on the trucks, the groups of Soldiers redeploying that day were loaded on buses and driven to the FOB's airfield. The enthusiasm was energizing as an occasional hoot and shout came from those going home. No one quieted or attempted to calm them down. There was no reason to. They had a right to do so after going through so much. It was time for them to go home.

As the buses were leaving the area, Kyle looked out of the window and saw the boulder where he used to smoke cigars and laugh with some of the enlisted Soldiers. There were a few guys hanging around, and it seemed like they were placing a new rock nearby. He then noticed that there were multiple painted rocks near the boulder that he hadn't seen before.

Kyle was suddenly internally torn with emotions. He was glad that he had started a tradition that would continue past his time in Iraq. At the same time, each new painted rock represented another life lost. Another Soldier who wouldn't enjoy the feeling of redeploying. Another loved one lost in the War on Terrorism. He easily spotted the rock that was placed in the area for Specialist Filner, and he almost became overwhelmed to the point of tears. Many stress-relieving sessions transpired at that large rock with smoking and talking. Filner sustained his injuries that eventually led to his death near that boulder, but the terrorist that had a large part in that attack had been captured. Kyle said a quick prayer for all of those that were deceased and for those who would face the same dangers in the following months.

The flight from Iraq to Kuwait was a rough one. The C-17 aircraft was hot and cramped. The flight was uncomfortable, but thankfully wasn't that long. They were placed into a small holding area while the bags and equipment were transferred to the contracted commercial plane headed for the United States.

After a couple of hours, the officer in charge of getting all of the passengers loaded on the airplane announced for the officers to come forward. After a quick count, he said, "Ok, you all get to sit in first class. Go ahead, grab your gear and proceed to the plane."

Kyle thought, *Damn, I ain't going to turn that down.* That was one of the times that he was going to use his rank to his advantage. He was happy to get the extra legroom for the long flight back.

He took a window seat and Chaplain Mosley sat next to him. He was also going home on the first redeployment flight since he had to be at Fort Stewart to receive the Soldiers coming back from 53rd Field Artillery. He had to be prepared to assist in any incidents that were typical during redeployments. One never knew who would have a bad reunion with their spouse or who couldn't let go of the anguish of being at war.

As the plane took off, the two friends were talking about how good it would be to sleep in their own beds and the reunion sex that would take place in them. Eventually, their fatigue took them out of the mood to chat and the conversation slowly ended. Chaplain Mosley dozed off, and Kyle pulled out his MP3 player. He scrolled through his playlists until he found his favorite tracks from the So So Def Bass All Stars, Volume II CD and closed his eyes. As the booty shake version of the Bell Biv Devoe hit *When Will I See Your Smile Again?* played, the reality of going home set in . . . he was going back to Georgia.

The airplane's touchdown at Wright Army Airfield was a remarkable homecoming. As the airplane taxied to its gate, pandemonium ensued inside the plane with a lot of hollering and hooting. On the outside, music blared and a firetruck sprayed the outside of the plane, perhaps as both a way of celebration and decontamination. Colorful banners and signs were waving behind a gated area near the main building on the airfield. Fellow Soldiers, family members, government officials, and friends of the men and women on the airplane could barely contain their excitement while they waited.

After the officer in charge made a few announcements everyone finally exited the plane. There was the red carpet again which led them to the receiving area. The Army band played patriotic tunes as a small unit of soldiers ushered them into the area. There were a series of quick welcome back speeches and a quick headcount before being officially released.

There was a rope and a few Soldiers that kept the crowd back. Kyle was searching the crowd for his parents. He didn't see them and became slightly concerned. He kept looking for them while all of the returning Soldiers were gathered in a formation. After a final count, the mayor of Savannah gave a brief welcome and was followed by the senior Fort Stewart chaplain.

After a couple more speakers, everyone was dismissed. The rope was dropped, and the crowd swarmed in to find their loved ones and friends. There were pockets of people everywhere with gifts or crying. Some people held their newborn children for the first time. Some people kissed their significant others or stayed in long, silent embraces. Kyle stood alone looking for his parents.

Nothing compares to the empty feeling of returning from a deployment and there's no one there to greet you. Looking at the "welcome back" signs and smiling families swiftly made Kyle sad. No one ran up to him to squeeze a hug, and no one screamed his name. Feeling snubbed, he played it off and headed in the direction of the bathroom. He pulled out his cell phone and pretended like he was engaged in a phone call. He wondered where his parents were because it wasn't like them to be late like that. He tried calling them a couple of times, but no one answered.

After a few minutes, he proceeded to head to the buses that would drop everyone off to their units. It wasn't mandatory to ride the bus back to the units, as long as they eventually made it to the unit to officially sign in.

Before Kyle made it to the front doors, he spotted his mother smiling and crying. He started crying as he ran to her and hugged her. His father showed up a minute later and hugged the both of them. At that moment, the deployment was finally over for Kyle.

His father cleared his throat and said, "Kyle, I'm sorry about our tardiness, but we have a surprise for you."

Kyle was hoping for a new car, but knowing how frugal his dad always was, he shunned the thought. They grabbed his bags and his mom said, "Let's get something to eat. I bet you are hungry."

As they walked toward his dad's Lincoln Towncar that was parked in a large field, Kyle saw Raven get out of the car. She was wearing the same yellow ribbon that she wore during his leave trip. Kyle stood frozen for a second not knowing how to react. Mr. Scott placed a hand on his son's shoulder and whispered, "LT Scott, you see why I was late, huh? How do you like my surprise? "

Kyle remained shocked for he did not expect to see Raven. Kyle's dad leaned in again and mentioned another surprise for him. He whispered to him that he had a suite in downtown Savannah for a few days for Kyle and Raven. The deal was that all of them had to have dinner first.

He laughed as he said, "Bust 'em in the head, son. Bust 'em in the head."

Epilogue

Jasper went from having multiple options for female companionship to basically none. There was no one that he wanted to call and invite over to hang with him on any given night. There was no one that he could kiss good morning and good night. He could definitely make a few phone calls if he had to in order to convince someone to come over occasionally, or he could mistakenly give the wrong one a chance to vie for his affection. He really wasn't in the mood for taking any chances or making more mistakes in love despite his occasional pang of loneliness. He missed genuine passion, which was part of the reason why he wasn't with any of his previous options.

Shelia would always be an occasional one night stand when both of them felt like it. It had become hit or miss with them as they placed other priorities or people in the mix of their lives. Even then, the times that they hooked up weren't as exciting as they used to be. Sonya was rumored to have a love interest that was making an honest bid for her free time and attention. They would always be friends who accepted that their past had no future. They were similar free spirits flowing in their own unaligned paths. Tara, his girlfriend before he was engaged to Tina, had started calling more. Given their past, it was still too awkward to have more than occasional conversations on the phone. The rest of Jasper's possibilities were lackluster or not worth his time. He didn't need any drama that could possibly come with them.

That night, Jasper contemplated his "war stories", as he called them….the fuck ups, the victories, the surprises, and the disappointments. Sitting in his living room, sipping beer alone while he listened to his library of self-made slow jam CDs, was commonplace and started to feel too comfortable. It was indeed comfy, but he also took that time alone to get to know himself and plot on his future business ideas. Always a forward thinker, Jasper felt that there was something more to himself than he could see.

He spoke to Kyle briefly upon his return, and they promised to catch up after he had a few days with his parents and Raven. After hanging up, *Lady* by the Whispers started playing, and Jasper turned up volume on the stereo. He enjoyed the vibe of the music. It was smooth, yet inspirational in some weird way. He grabbed another beer, his notebook from the coffee table and jotted down various hustle ideas.

Kyle woke up the next day to the sound of his phone alerting him in succession that he had a multiple voicemails and texts. According to the log of missed calls, most of them came from his mother. He rolled out of bed slowly and read the first few texts. His mom wanted him and Raven to stop by the hotel that his parents were staying to have dinner again that night. He assumed that Raven agreed to do so plan based on the exchange of the words on his screen between her and his mom. He felt tired and dehydrated from romping with her the night before.

As he heard the water from the shower turn off, he placed the phone back on the nightstand. *I'll read them later.* Moments later, Raven appeared drying herself off as she walked around the hotel room looking for various items like her underwear and deodorant. Kyle watched in silence as her hips swung and her breasts bounced with each stride. She was startled when she realized that Kyle was awake and out of bed looking at her.

"Oh shit baby! Don't do that shit. I thought you were still sleep." Raven continued grabbing underwear and the toiletries that she needed before heading back to the bathroom. Kyle followed and slapped her on the ass before he went to pee. They talked as she got dressed, and he brushed his teeth.

The conversation was random, sprinkled with recaps of their physical reunion and what they wanted to do for the day. Kyle was pleased with how comfortable he was with her. He was even more ecstatic that his father made peace with his decision to date her and chose not to meddle so much into his life – personal or professional.

"So what time do you want to go your parents' hotel to eat?" Raven was trying to get her boyfriend to stop shuffling around and to get moving. "Do you want to go to the movies first or after?"

Kyle was still tired and just wanted to enjoy the fact that he was finally home from the war. The hot days, the long hours, the heartaches, and the nightmares were finally over.

"Baby, I really don't want to go anywhere. Actually, I kinda wanna just chill."

Raven understood, but she still wanted to get out to see the area around Fort Stewart. "Well, ok. So, umm . . . whatcha wanna do?" As she said that, she kicked off her shoes anticipating that she and Kyle weren't going anywhere anytime soon.

"Hmmm. Perhaps we can convince my mom to cook something. There are a few plates, pans, and utensils here in the hotel room."

Raven was down to do whatever as long as Kyle was ok. She missed him and was glad for the second chance. She promised herself and his dad that she would always have his back. Raven sat back on the bed.

"If that is what you want, then I can cook something and invite them over. What do you want?"

Kyle smirked and in his naturally deep voice said, "Umm. I think that I want some of your pepper steak."

Rodney was up past one in the morning listening to various songs by Con Funk Shun in his garage. With his bass guitar in his lap and headphones hanging around his neck, he strummed the bassline to the first song that he ever attempted to play on one of his father's guitars. The volume of "I'm Leaving Baby" was low enough for him to hear the notes he played that came from his amplifier, but loud enough to miss Katrina walking in.

His head was throbbing as he kept rewinding the last couple of minutes to figure out the fingering variations for the bassline of the last minute or so of the song. Frustrated about fumbling it each time, he cursed audibly before he stopped, closed his eyes, took a deep breath, and hit the rewind button.

His wife just stood there watching him get lost in his moment. Katrina walked up behind him and tapped him softly and stepped back. He jumped when he was broken from his daze. She yawned as she walked away and said, "Come on, baby. You need to come to bed. We have church in the morning."

"Ok. I will be in there in a minute. I almost got that part of the song, and . . .," as Rodney was explaining he yawned.

Exhausted, Katrina said, "Ok, I was going to give you some, but I'm tired now. I'm going to bed."

Rodney sat back down and rewound the CD to make another attempt before calling it quits. The time to leave for church was going to come quick, and he needed to be on top of his game. Even though it was an easy gig for him, it helped him meet ends financially. As he fumbled the bassline again, he closed his eyes and took a couple of deep breaths before starting over.

Acknowledgements

Dante D. Long would like to thank:

I would like to thank my two beautiful children for you were the motivation for every hustle and success that I have ever had since you were both born.

As always, I would like to thank the two other "Men of 1302". Your personalities and our experiences in college inspired some of the characters, this book, and the whole series to come. I love both of you brothers.

I have to give a special thank you to everyone who had a hand in making this dream of becoming an author come true, no matter how big or small. Each and every phone call, proofreading, motivational word, honest feedback, and ideas that I may have gotten from all of you are much appreciated. I apologize for not naming each person on this page, but there are so many that helped to make this possible. Your support all these years means so much to me.

I have to give a special shout out to all of the authors and others in the publishing industry that ever gave consultation, advice, and kind words.

Dark Diamond Publishing, LLC.

Check us out and follow us at

www.darkdiamondbooks.com
www.facebook.com/DarkDiamondPublishing
www.twitter.com/dd_publishing
www.instagram.com/dark_diamond_publishing

Read excerpts and subscribe to the newsletter. Stay tuned
to future developments from Dante D. Long and Dark
Diamond Publishing

Dante D. Long
www.facebook.com/authordante.long
www.twitter.com/authordantelong

About Dante D. Long

Dante D. Long is a native of Georgia and currently residing in the Midwest. *The Soul's Motivation* is his second novel and the second of the *Men of 1302* series. He is also a contributing blogger for the Onyx Truth website and the host of the Southern Soulcast podcast. He is currently working on various projects including the third *Men of 1302* novel.

Learn more about Dante D. Long at

www.darkdiamondbooks.com/author_dante.html

Check out the blog posts of Dante D. Long and episodes of the Southern Soulcast podcast at www.onyxtruth.com